What people are saying abou g

"Overall, Sister Margaret is a short, quick, gritty read that's a wonderful start to this new series by the Myers siblings with its intriguing characters, nice sense of urgency, and satisfying conclusion."
-Zoe Williams. 8/10 Stars whatsbetterthanbooks.com -Best Book Blog 2017

"Sister Margaret is a slam dunk police procedural, giving the most on-the-money insider view of an investigation"…"if you are on the lookout for a new series of gritty police procedurals then Travis Myers and Natasha Myers Marsiguerra are definitely names to watch."
-DeathBecomesHer. crimefictionlover.com

"This really is a well-written novel that was an enjoyable and highly entertaining read."
-Nursebookie. 5/5 Stars Goodreads

"I really enjoyed this book! With just under 200 pages you have a fast-paced plot, fully developed characters, and a wild glimpse into the life of an NYPD detective…I would suggest grabbing a copy of this book!"
-Brianas_best_reads. 5/5 Stars Goodreads

"The first book of the Tommy Keane series did NOT disappoint…I would definitely recommend this to anyone who loves a good police procedural."
-Laura's Reviews. 5/5 stars Goodreads

"This little gem of a novel…feels as though it could have been ripped right out of the newspapers"
-Kelly_Kills_Books. 5/5 Stars Goodreads

"Finished Sister Margaret and loved it so much! It gave me total *Law & Order* vibes…I absolutely cannot wait for book two"
Britt the Bookworm. 5/5 Stars Goodreads

"Exactly what I want from a Crime/Detective story…Yes, I would recommend this to anyone who likes police procedurals, and crime fiction.
Sean's page. 5/5 Stars Goodreads

"One of the most intriguing, intense and suspenseful novels I have read in a long time."
Alison Owen. 5/5 Stars Goodreads

"Suspenseful and action packed! The writing is tight and the characters ring true. Highly recommended!"
Giuliana D. 5/5 Stars Amazon

"A Nun is brutally murdered…and what is discovered is much more disturbing than the murder itself…This is one of my favorite books of the year"
Killer-K. 5/5 Stars Barnes & Noble

"Very Authentic! What a great read. I was hooked from the start. Cannot wait for the next in the series!
Betty Book Page 5/5 Stars Barnes & Noble.

"Great Detective novel…This is a must read for fans of crime fiction"
Tina Jackson 5/5 Stars Books A Million

HAYDEN JON MARSHALL

Also by Travis Myers
&
Natasha Myers Marsiguerra

Sister Margaret

HAYDEN JON MARSHALL

A Tommy Keane Novel

Travis Myers &
Natasha Myers Marsiguerra

Hayden Jon Marshall is a work of fiction. Names, characters, and incidents are the product of the author's imagination and are used fictitiously. Any resemblance to actual events, or persons, living or dead, is entirely coincidental.

Published in the United States by Bully Press Corp.

Bully Press Corp
P. O. Box 404
Wingdale, NY 12594 United States
 www.bullypress.net

Cover design by: Phred Rawles

ISBN-13: 978-1-7343370-3-7

For the clean-up team:

Mary, Rosemarie, Christine, Henry, and Kristina.

***

Dedicated to every Cop and Detective, in every city, in every country on the planet. Thank you for standing on the side of right, and for fighting the good and never-ending fight against those who would destroy all we hold dear.

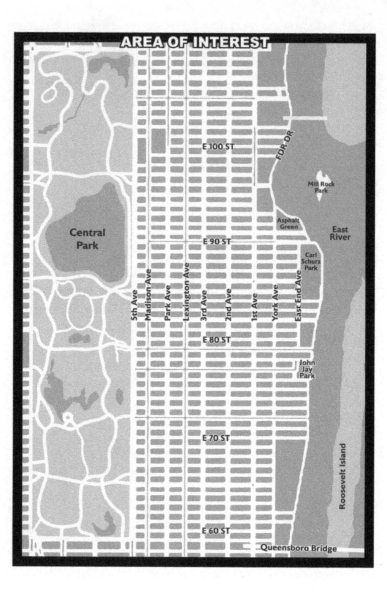

"When a child goes missing, the whole world stops."

~Sergeant John Dolan, 52nd Precinct, the Bronx

Prologue

Tommy Keane had been a Detective in the 53rd Precinct Detective Squad, in the Bronx, for just over two weeks when he caught his first missing person's case.

Eight-year-old Mariana Castro disappeared from the lobby of her building on 196th Street and Valentine Avenue, sometime around 3:50 PM on a warm Wednesday afternoon in April.

The call came into the squad about the missing girl, and Keane, along with Detective Bobby O'Reilly, responded to the scene within 15 minutes of receiving the notification. Upon their arrival Sgt. Timothy McColl and Police Officer Denise Brenan informed the two detectives of the details they had received from the hysterical mother, one Idina Castro, 32, and her equally upset twelve-year-old son, Jose Castro.

The detectives climbed the stairs of the building and went to the family's third story apartment and knocked on the door. Upon entering, Tommy immediately took note of the surroundings, as his eyes scanned the room. The apartment was immaculate -- spotless hardwood floors, and pure white walls throughout the two-bedroom apartment. Mrs. Castro motioned toward the sitting area, and Tommy sat on the edge of the black leather sofa, set against the wall of the living room.

He took note of various black framed photos of the family and grade school photos of both children on the spotless glass end tables and coffee table. There was a 43-inch Sony flat screen television directly across from the sofa, and on the side wall a large wedding photo of Idina and her husband hung below a large black and silver crucifix.

Mrs. Castro, through her panic and tears, immediately offered the detectives coffee as they sat down to interview her and her son, which both detectives graciously declined.

"No ma'am, Mrs. Castro. We are fine. We are going to ask you about your daughter so we can get to work finding her as quickly as we possibly can. Okay?"

Tommy and Detective O'Reilly instantly knew this was a good family, or at least that Idina Castro was an attentive mother, who kept her home and children well cared for. They learned her husband, Victor Castro, worked for UPS and was currently on his way home. He left work early as soon as he had learned his daughter was missing.

Idina sat in one of the chairs, her son Jose standing just slightly behind her. He was wearing a faded Batman t-shirt and continuously grabbed at the hem, wringing and tugging at it nervously.

"When did you realize your daughter Mariana was missing, Mrs. Castro?" Tommy asked.

Through her tears, she looked at Tommy and nervously answered, her hands shaking. "Aye," she exclaimed, "She and Jose just came home from school and they, they went downstairs to get the mail from the, from the mailbox. They get the mail from the box in the lobby most days after they come home from school."

"So, Jose, you were with Mariana?" Detective O'Reilly asked.

"Yes," he said through his tears, "but I ran up the stairs ahead of her, I don't know why. I ran just to be, just to be stupid and be funny. I ran up the stairs while she was getting the mail... I don't know why."

"How long was she alone in the lobby?" Tommy asked.

"I don't even know, maybe a minute, maybe two before I went to go to look for her... I called for her and thought she was maybe hiding under the stairs, you know to be stupid and playing stupid games, you know... I called for her, and looked for her and called for her but she didn't answer. I went to the street and looked up and down and into the alley between the buildings, then I came back in the lobby and called for her again and told her to stop being stupid but she didn't answer me."

"Is that when you told your mother and she called the police, Jose?"

"Yes, I looked and looked and then got scared, like you know... like really scared. I got scared and told Mommy," he said through his tears.

"We have officers and detectives looking all over the building and all over the neighborhood right now," Tommy said in as comforting a voice as he could muster.

"Now, is there anything that you can think of about how she was dressed, or where she may have gone, maybe to a friend's or a relative's house? Does she have any friends in the building or close by in the neighborhood? Do you have any relatives close by, any place you can think of she may have gone?" Tommy asked.

"Aye, I don't know...yes. She has a friend upstairs on the fourth floor, Tina, but no friends or family close...not close. Like maybe ten blocks away... but she, she, Mariana wouldn't walk there herself... I don't think she would ever do that. She is a good girl, and she is a home girl. She would never leave the building on her own," Idina said, still physically shaking.

"Okay, well please give me all the names and places where she has, or may have, a friend or a relative. And relax, Mrs. Castro, we're going to find Mariana, or hopefully she'll come walking through that door any minute. That's usually the case, dear. Hopefully she's at a friend's or still thinks she's playing a joke on Jose... But we'll find her. I promise," Tommy said. Then he thought to himself, 'God, I hope I'm right.'

The interview went on a bit longer and a missing-persons report was filled out. Within minutes every car in the precinct and adjoining precincts had a description of little Mariana and each of them were on the lookout for her.

***

There were 32 apartments in the Castro's building and each and every door was knocked on -- nineteen of them were answered and the occupants questioned. Most were shocked and surprised to hear that little Mariana had disappeared from their lobby, none more so than her little friend Tina's mother on the fourth floor, who immediately became hysterical and was inconsolable for several minutes after hearing the news. Everyone in the building who knew the family repeated the same sentiment and confirmed Keane and O'Reilly's initial feelings, that this was indeed a solid loving family who took care of their children.

The detectives and assisting patrol officers thoroughly searched the building, including the roof, basement and adjoining alleyways and backyards.

The building's superintendent, Juan Rodriguez, gave the detectives a tenants list, which contained the names and some phone numbers of the occupants of each apartment. He also told the detectives that the Castro's were a fine hard-working family who loved their children, and that they were liked by everyone on the block. According to Rodriguez they had lived in the building for about ten years and there had never been a problem with them. He also went on to say that there were no drugs in the building. "None of that drug shit here," he emphatically repeated, "I keep that shit out of this building."

Both Detectives worked well past their shift that night, interviewing as many people in the building as they were able to find. They spoke to neighbors on the block, the pizzeria and the bodega across the street, as well as every other business that was open within a two- to three-block radius of the Castro's building, all with no luck. No one had seen Mariana or noticed anything suspicious.

When Victor Castro returned home, they also interviewed him extensively. He certainly wasn't a suspect in their minds. Both detectives knew he was at work during Mariana's disappearance. They also knew he adored his daughter and by all accounts was an excellent father and family man. But both men, being excellent detectives, would leave no question unasked and no rock unturned in their search for little Mariana.

***

The following day's shift brought more of the same and greater worry for Mariana Castro's wellbeing. Nothing had been found in the detectives' search for this little girl. Not a single clue had shown itself to either Keane or the older, more experienced O'Reilly.

Both men went over every interview, both in their heads and with each other. They again canvassed the neighborhood. They went to Mariana's school and spoke with her teachers and her principal, and they spoke with her friends and her school mates. But after a full day of searching, plus another several hours of overtime, Tommy Keane again had nothing to go on.

***

05:04 AM Friday Morning:

Tommy received a call on his cell phone from Juan Rodriguez, the super of Mariana's building. He was obviously very shaken and sounded frantic on the phone. He told Tommy he needed to come to the building right away. He had just found Mariana's lifeless body in the building's alleyway.

Tommy instructed Mr. Rodriguez to touch nothing, to let absolutely no one enter the alley, and to tell no one what he had found. He told him that the police would arrive very soon. He then called the station and told them to send a patrol car over to secure the crime scene. Then, he called Bobby O'Reilly and told him about the call.

He headed out the door and drove about 90 miles an hour, straight from his home in Brewster, New York to the building on 196th Street and Valentine Avenue. Tommy made the trip to the Bronx in less than 40 minutes.

He arrived at the building at 5:58 AM. There, he met Sgt. Kim Myrnnanski, who stood guard over the alleyway with three other police officers from patrol. When Tommy greeted her, she said with a tear in her eye, "She's in the alley… The super found her this morning, he told me he called you. You'll find her over there."

Sgt. Myrnnanski pointed, "She's in the trash can. Whatever fucking savage did this, put her in a trash bag and stuck her in that trash can over there."

"Ahh, fuck me," Tommy replied, with gut-wrenching angst.

"I put in a call to Crime Scene and the Medical Examiner already," Myrnnanski stated.

"The super?" Tommy asked.

"I have him in the car," she replied, "I didn't want him talking to anyone before you showed up."

"Good job, Sarge," he replied. Then he stepped a bit closer and asked in a lower, almost fearful tone, "And the parents?"

"We haven't spoken to anyone, Detective. I wanted you to handle this your way."

"So, so do they know yet?"

"No sir, not to my knowledge."

At that time Bobby O'Reilly pulled up and got out of his car. He had also just driven straight in from his home in Pearl River, New York.

"Is it her? Is it Mariana?" He asked with dread, anticipating the awful answer.

"I haven't looked yet… I just got here myself, but the super said it was. And the Sergeant here says the body is here, in a trash can in the alley," Tommy replied.

"Ah fuck, no, no, no, don't tell me that!" O'Reilly exclaimed.

The detectives walked the 60 or so feet down the narrow alley to where the trash from the building was stacked to go out that morning. They went up to the banged-up, grey metal can which had a black plastic garbage bag in it. The top was open and partially folded back, and inside, folded up into a tight fetal position, was the naked little battered body of Mariana Castro.

Both men stood side by side and stared. They stared for no longer than a minute, but for both men, it felt like an eternity. The only things visible at that moment were the top of Mariana's head, the right side of her obviously beaten face, her bruised and battered bare shoulders, and the tops of her bruised knees. Neither man spoke, and neither man moved for that moment.

Keane and O'Reilly wanted to do something, but knew they couldn't. They had to leave little Mariana exactly where she was, and exactly as she was, until Crime Scene and the Medical Examiner showed up. Both of which could take hours.

Both men silently steeled themselves in preparation for the tasks they had ahead of them. The first task was to notify the parents, who at this moment were probably in their apartment, less than 100 feet from where the detectives now stood looking at little Mariana. They would need to interview the super, and then abandon this missing person's case in search of the answers to this new homicide case, the one which began with a trash can, in the alley they both stood in, at approximately 6:26 AM on an otherwise beautifully warm Friday morning in April.

***

O'Reilly asked, "You alright, Tom?"

"Yep," Tommy replied in a low voice. His answer was yes, but his rigid stance and the dead pan and determined look on his face said otherwise.

"I'm gonna call the Lu now and let him know what's up, and see if we can get a couple more guys over here," O'Reilly said.

"Yeah, do that. I'm gonna get the super, Juan. What do you think? We'll go to his apartment for the interview?... And I guess, fuck, I guess we should go tell Mr. & Mrs. Castro now?" Tommy asked, already regretting every minute of this day which was yet to come.

"Yeah, let's get Juan into his apartment and interview him, and let's get a uniform up in front of the Castros' door to make sure they stay in there until we go talk to them. Hopefully they won't be lookin' to leave for work anytime soon. I'd really rather we got Crime Scene done and had the body removed, if possible. Fuck, I hope those fucks get here soon," O'Reilly said.

"Good thinking, Bobby," Tommy replied. Then he found Sgt. Myrnnanski and asked her, "Please post a uniformed officer in front of the Castros' door, and in the event anyone wants to leave, tell them to stay inside and wait until we arrive… Don't tell them anything other than we are on the way and won't be long."

"Okay, got it," she replied.

***

Inside Juan Rodriguez' apartment, his story was short and simple.

"I got up this morning about 4:45. I went to do the garbage. You know, today is garbage day, so I got to pull it all out of the alley and take it out to the curb. So I drag out a couple of bags and the first two cans. Then I try to drag the third can but can't. I say, 'Damn, this one is heavy.' So I, then I, I opened the bag." His tears began to flow. "I see her…that beautiful girl, I see her, I see her… Then I try to be strong and I call your number right away, Detective…right away. I don't touch nothing else. I don't tell no one, not a soul and I stand here in the alley till those police show up…and no one came in until I show those cops there who came…that woman Sergeant and her partner that are there now. That's it, nobody else, no one."

"You did good, Juan. You did real good. We can't thank you enough for your help," Tommy said in a sympathetic voice. "You know, we're going to have to ask you a lot more questions today, but we have so many things to do first. So I'd like to ask you to stay right here at home, to please just sit tight, talk to no one about this -- not your family, no friends, no phone calls until we get back to you. Can I ask you to do that for us, just hang tight for a couple hours?"

"Yes, anything, anything you need. Anything you want from me, Detective, I will do anything," Juan replied, as he began to tear up again.

There was a knock on the door.

O'Reilly answered it and a Patrol Officer said, in a whisper, "Crime Scene is here."

"Thanks, pal," O'Reilly replied. "Tommy…Crime Scene is outside."

Tommy gave the super a squeeze on his shoulder and exited the apartment. He and O'Reilly stepped out of the building and met with the crime scene team. They quickly gave a synopsis of what they knew, as the Crime Scene Investigators got started with the photographing, measuring, and searching for forensic evidence. They quickly dusted the trash can for fingerprints then nodded to the detectives that they could remove Mariana's body. They tried to pull her out by the trash bag, which gave way and tore due to the weight of the body. Tommy tightened his lips, curling them in on themselves, again trying to steel himself to the situation at hand.

As Tommy's heart broke at the sight of little Mariana, he gently placed his hands under Mariana's arms, and with the help of one the crime scene detectives, who put his hands behind her knees, they pulled her little limp body from the can, the bag still wrapped around her. They carefully placed her on a sheet that had been laid out for her on the warm concrete sidewalk of the alley.

"She's limp," the Crime Scene Detective said, "I'm going to guess she's been dead for more than a day, but you gotta wait for the M.E. to tell you that."

Tommy and Bobby O'Reilly stood silent as the photographer took his photos, then they cut and removed the plastic bag from around her body.

"Fucking motherfuckers!" The Crime Scene Officer exclaimed.

Marianas small body lay in front of the five men who encircled her. Her hair was still in a ponytail, and she was completely naked but for a pair of red Skippy sneakers and white ankle socks, with red trim and a little red fuzzy pom pom on the back of each one. Her body was covered in bruises. There were deep cuts on her head and cheek bone, and dozens of obvious bite marks all over her body and limbs.

All five men stood frozen in this moment, knowing the image before them was something they would never be able to wash from their memories.

The photographer continued to take his photographs, then gave his partner a nod and he and Tommy gently flipped little Mariana's body so the rest of her corpse could be photographed and examined.

At this time, the Medical Examiner came walking down the alleyway. Both Tommy and Bobby recognized her as Angela Marcus. Cops who knew her referred to her as the Vampire, because she had this otherworldly, almost immortal quality about her, and because she worked in the world of the dead. She was tall, thin, always very well dressed, with short, slicked back blonde hair that gave her a bit of a David Bowie look, especially today in her impeccably tailored cream colored pant suit and matching pumps. Although she was quite attractive, she was always very sullen, and she never smiled.

As she approached she showed her I.D. and said flatly, "Morning, Detectives. Marcus, Medical Examiner's office."

She squatted next to the body, creating an even stranger image -- this tall, well-dressed, strangely attractive woman in high heels donning her blue latex gloves, then physically examining the young broken body that lay before her.

She lifted Mariana's limbs, looked inside her mouth, touched and prodded her little body everywhere. Then she asked the detectives to flip her, and she continued to do a cursory examination of Mariana's entire body. The process took no more than four minutes total.

She stood over the body and as she removed her gloves she looked up at Tommy, with her ice blue eyes, and said very flatly, "She's dead. She appears to have been beaten to death, most probably with fists. I don't see any outright signs of forced sex, but I'm not going to rule that out until we do a complete work up on her at the morgue. As of right now I don't think she was raped, and as for all of these bite marks, I believe they were made both prior to, and after death. Again, that's my assumption, you'll have to wait for my full report… I'm going to guess this happened sometime between 24 and 36 hours ago. Which one of you is the case detective?"

Tommy raised his hand, "Right here, Tommy Keane 5-3 Squad."

"Here's my card, Detective. May I have yours please?"

He pulled one out and handed it to her. "Thank you," he said as he gave her his card.

"Don't thank me, Detective, I'm just doing my job, same as you. Good luck catching this animal. Hopefully you'll have whoever did this before we see each other again."

The five men stood and watched her walk back out of the alley. The two M.E. Techs were waiting at the end of the alley with a stretcher to take the body. Once they received the okay from the detectives, they placed Mariana's body into a body bag and carried her away from the scene.

***

9:15 AM

Time-wise, things were moving rather quickly. Tommy and Bobby O'Reilly credited that to Sgt. Myrnnanski for putting in the call to Crime Scene, and alerting them to the situation. That, and the early hour, helped get things rolling. The Crime Scene Unit continued to poke around the alley, looking for anything that could be important. Tommy and Bobby decided to allow the M.E.'s office to remove the body to the morgue.

Although it would have been more convenient to bring Mr. and Mrs. Castro downstairs to identify their daughter's body, both detectives felt it would be better to see their daughter's body in a more clinical setting, like the morgue, than here in the alley amongst the trash, or in the Medical Examiner's meat wagon.

The detectives then made the longest walk any detective ever has to make. They climbed the stairs to tell Idina and Victor Castro that their daughter was dead.

When they arrived at the third floor apartment, they asked the uniform at the door if he had spoken to anyone.

"Yes, the father -- the husband, I think, came out, and I told him just what you said, just to wait for you," the officer replied.

"And what did he say?" Bobby O'Reilly asked.

"He said, 'Okay.' He didn't look so good. Then he opened the door and asked if I wanted to come in and sit, or if I wanted some coffee. I said 'No thank you.'"

"What time?" Tommy asked.

"Bout 15, maybe 20 minutes ago," the officer replied.

Tommy gently knocked on the door. It slowly opened and both Victor and Idina stood looking out of the eight-inch opening, with Victor looking over Idina's head. Seeing the two detectives, they opened the door fully.

After no more than three or four seconds of eye contact, Idina cried out "No...No!" and her knees buckled. Victor caught her, as she let her body fall towards the floor. Tommy leaned in to help catch Idina, as she cried out and went limp.

Victor looked into Tommy's eyes, his own filling with water. "No, don't say it," Victor said in the desperate fear and sadness only a parent would recognize.

"I'm sorry," Tommy said in a low voice, his eyes also filling up.

Idina screamed out again, "No! No!" She flailed her legs while her husband Victor restrained her in his arms.

Keane and O'Reilly entered the apartment, and they all slowly moved into the living room, where they had had their initial meeting.

"Please sit," Detective O'Reilly said, "There are no words we can say to express our sorrow. We found her this morning. She was killed probably very soon after she had gone missing on Wednesday, but we're not sure yet. I want you...we want you, to take some time to gather yourselves, then we'll take one of you to the hospital to identify her body."

"Identify the body?" Victor said with a glimmer of hope, "Is it possible...could you be wrong, maybe?"

"No, Mr. Castro," Tommy said, reaching out and putting his hand on Victor's forearm, "It's Mariana."

Both parents openly wept, hiding their heads in one another's shoulders.

"Listen," Tommy began, "We have to go to work now to find out what happened and who did this. You have our numbers and we have yours. When you think you are able, we'll come back and take you for the I.D. Please just stay here, just just stay here at home, love each other...and that beautiful boy of yours. And I want you to know -- you have to know this. Listen to me, Mrs. Castro, Mr. Castro. Whatever happened to Mariana is not your fault and you have to let your boy Jose know that it is not his fault. Please hear me now, a bad person did something bad, we'll find out who, and that's the only person who has to answer for this. Do you understand? Do you hear what I am telling you? The only person to blame is the evil fucker that did this bad thing, and I promise you we will find them."

His face still buried in his wife's neck, Victor Castro spoke, "Thank you, Detectives. Thank you."

"We'll talk soon," Bobby replied.

And then both men exited the apartment.

"Hang here for a bit more," Tommy said to the uniform as they left the apartment.

***

The detectives made their way down the marble steps to the lobby -- Tommy more hastily and purposefully than O'Reilly, whose pace was somewhat hampered by the drama of the morning. When they reached the lobby door, Tommy spoke out, "Okay…Let me think for a minute."

Bobby O'Reilly stared at him.

Tommy began, "She never left the building…It happened here. Whatever happened, whoever did this, it happened here. Not in this lobby, but in this building." He headed for the door.

Sergeant Myrnnanski had been relieved and there were two new officers at the alleyway.

"Do us a favor, Bobby. Call the Lu, have him send over a couple of guys from the squad and a couple more uniforms. We're going back through this building, one apartment at a time," Tommy said.

"Hey, Tom, you know we gotta--" Bobby began, but Tommy cut him off.

"Give me a minute, I gotta think for a minute… Make that call, please."

Bobby O'Reilly made the call as Tommy stepped back into the lobby.

When Bobby finished the call, he found Tommy in the center of the lobby, staring at the rows of mailboxes on the wall.

Bobby stood silently and looked at Tommy; he could see the wheels in his brain were turning.

"Okay Bobby… She was here, and then she wasn't. No one we spoke to saw her outside of this building, so I say…I say she never left. I say this fucking savage killed this little girl right here, right fucking here and fuck me, fuck me, possibly while we were here looking for her. Listen, just listen now, let me get it out… We knocked on every door but not everyone answered. We ran everyone on that list that Juan gave us, but nothing came back that interested us, so we looked elsewhere, didn't we? We looked at her school, we checked the other buildings… No, no, no, no, that fucker, that dirty fucker, did this here. He tortured her, and he killed her right here, probably that day. She was probably dead just minutes or hours after we arrived if not before we arrived. And today, fucking today is trash day, so he stuck that beautiful little girl in a black garbage bag and put her in the trash where Juan found her. Stick your head out that door, Bobby, tell me if we have more people here yet.

Bobby O'Reilly stepped out the front door onto the street, then opened it back up and shouted to Tommy, "Uniforms just pulled up."

Tommy walked outside and called the four uniformed patrol officers together.

"Listen guys, we think we may have a perp inside this building in one of the apartments. What I want you guys to do, is each take a corner of the building. You two head down the alley and one of you go down to the far corner of the courtyard. You two wait here outside, one on either side of the building. Keep your eyes on the fire escapes and the front door. It's a pretty far jump from one roof to another on this block, but I've seen perps clear alleyways wider than these like fuckin gazelles. If that happens, let us know, follow them, catch them. This is a bad evil fucker we're after, so if you see anybody leave this place and they aren't with us, you stop them, and if they're running you be sure to grab them."

"You got it," one of the officers replied.

Bobby asked, "You wanna wait for our guys or you wanna get started now, Tom?"

"I don't think I can wait, man. We gotta get this fucker."

"Okay," Bobby replied, "I'm with you."

Both detectives reentered the building, and Tommy called up to the third floor, to where the other uniformed officer was still standing, outside of the Castros' apartment.

Tommy began, "Listen, my partner and I think our perp is here in the building. We're going to go apartment by apartment to find him. We got uniformed guys outside watching the roof, the fire escapes, and the front door. You, my friend, are gonna be our backup. Each apartment we enter, you're gonna stand outside, or in the stairwell, and keep an eye out and an ear open in case anyone tries to get out of this building. Anyone outside of an 80 year-old abuela comes out of any of these apartments and we're not out here, you stop them, you got that?"

"Yes, sir, I got it," the officer replied.

"Good man," Tommy said. "Okay, Bobby, we hit most of these apartments. So let's start right here on the first floor and see what we have. I think we were both satisfied with 1A and 1C. We didn't get any answer from 1B or 1D, so let's start with D since it's the closest to us and to these mailboxes."

Tommy knocked on the door, and then knocked again. A tall black man of about 70, wearing boxer shorts and a robe, answered the door, smoking a cigarette.

"Yes? You the police? I hear you making some noise outside this morning, what can I do for you all?"

"Yes, sir, I'm Detective O'Reilly and this is my partner, Detective Keane. We would like to--"

"Okay, yeah you there, Detective Keane, you left your card in my door. What can I do for you, Detectives? I like to help the police, but I gotta tell you I don't know nothing, I haven't seen nothing, and I can't hardly hear, so I know I ain't heard nothing."

"Can we step inside, sir?" Bobby asked.

"Sure, come on in Detectives, I'm sorry my place isn't very tidy. My wife died some ten years ago and she was in charge of the cleaning."

"That's alright sir, we're looking for a missing girl who..."

"You're looking for that pretty little Puerto Rican girl from the third floor? She still ain't come home yet? Shit that ain't good... I don't think I can help you, but if you need to look around go ahead. She ain't here. Nice girl, nice family, but she sure wouldn't be in here."

"Let me ask you, Mr.--" Tommy started to ask.

"Name's Reynolds, Reggie Wright Reynolds...spell it with a Y."

"Let me ask you, Mr. Reynolds... I know you say you don't hear or see much these days, but something tells me you're a sharp fella, maybe sharper than you like to let on. Who in this building, do you think, could possibly hurt a child?"

"Hurt a child? You think somebody in this building hurt that child?" Mr. Reynolds became agitated, "Well, I'll tell you right away, only one motherfucker comes to this old man's mind... We got a good building here, a good building with good people, but there's this sweet Puerto Rican girl who lives across the hall in the B line -- that's apartment 1B right across the lobby -- and she has a crazy as hell little brother, maybe 22 or 23 years old. That boy is crazy. I seen him kick a cat across the street like it was a football one time...no reason, just mean! He don't look right either. If you look at him you know that boy ain't right."

"1B huh, Mr. Reynolds? Well, we'll be sure to check on him," Bobby replied, "Thank you for your time, sir."

Both detectives shook his hand.

"Good luck boys and be careful. I'm tellin you that boy is crazy."

As Mr. Reynolds closed his apartment door, Keane and O'Reilly walked directly across the lobby, to apartment 1B.

Bobby asked Tommy, "We don't have a warrant, how do you want to play this?"

"Hopefully someone comes to the door. We have no idea if this is our guy, we'll just have to play it by ear and see what happens." Tommy replied.

Tommy knocked on the door gently, and motioned to the uniformed officer to get back away from view of the door. They each removed their pistols from their holsters. No answer, so Tommy knocked again. The door slowly opened and an attractive young woman slipped out into the hallway.

She was about five feet tall, barefoot, in red panties, and a tight grey T shirt. She looked up at Tommy and O'Reilly with a dazed and confused look, one of her eyes blackened.

She whispered to Tommy, "I've been waiting for you. He's in bed, he's out cold. He been drinkin and druggin all night. He's who you're looking for. What took you so long? ... What took you so long? I been waiting for you for so long," she repeated, standing half-naked in the doorway of the apartment, as her hands and knees shook.

The detectives briefly made eye contact in disbelief.

"Where is he?" Tommy asked.

"Bedroom, in the bedroom, second door on the right," she muttered.

"Anyone else in the apartment?" Bobby whispered.

"Nah, just him. Out cold, he's out cold in the bedroom, second door on the right. Please... don't shoot him," she said, "He's my brother."

Tommy gently pulled the young woman out into the lobby, and both detectives entered the apartment, with their pistols drawn. Tommy led the way, slowly moving toward the door. Reaching across it, he slowly and quietly turned the knob and opened it.

And there he was, lying face down in bed, fast asleep with nothing on but a pair of SpongeBob boxer shorts. Tommy put a finger over his lips to O'Reilly, holstered his weapon and removed his cuffs. Then he leapt onto the man in bed, cuffing one wrist while digging his knee into the man's back, and then cuffing the second. The man screamed like a banshee with fear, he had no chance to resist.

Tommy flipped the man onto the floor and Bobby turned the lights on. The two detectives stood there awestruck.

With the lights on, they could see blood all over the sheets and little Mariana's clothing on the floor. There was no doubt this was their man, or that this was where Mariana had died.

The man, 24 year-old Pedro Padilla, looked up at Tommy, who stood over his small, almost-naked body, and he smiled up at him. Then, with a happy lilt to his voice he said, "Fuck you, pig, you're too fucking late."

Tommy instantly filled with rage. He punched Pedro hard on the side of the head with his left hand, then pulled his pistol from his holster and raised it to Pedro's head. Bobby O'Reilly shouted in a strong clear voice, "Tommy, No!"

Tommy just froze. "If you kill him, we'll have to answer for it, and if we beat him, we'll look bad in court. No, Tommy. We got him, we got him, and we got him cold. Let them rape and kill his ass in Sing Sing," he said, changing his focus from Tommy, and staring deep into Pedro Padilla's eyes. "Let them rape him, and let him die a miserable death there."

The apartment was less than 30 feet from the mailboxes, and it had taken less than eight seconds for Pedro Padilla to snatch up little Mariana from the lobby and secret her in his sister's apartment.

Later at the station house, it was all every cop and every detective could do, not to tear Pedro Padilla apart. They treated him as poorly as possible, without getting physical. The only time he wasn't rear cuffed was when he was printed. No matter how many times he asked to be uncuffed, they stayed on. Every man and woman in the precinct wanted to beat him to death, but no one dared jeopardize a case like this. No, Bobby O'Reilly was right, if ever there was a demon who deserved some street justice, it was this one.

So they all took charge of their emotions, and in as professional a manner as they could muster, they processed Pedro Padilla for the savage murder of Mariana Castro.

***

Every detective, every cop in every city in the world, has a ghost that never lets them go, a reminder of their own frailty and weakness. Some victim they couldn't save or avenge. Mariana Castro was one of Tommy Keane's many ghosts, a sweet innocent girl whose family gave her a chance at a good life, at a better life than most, and who, through no fault of her own, no fault of her parents, or her older brother, had that chance stolen from her by an evil, twisted degenerate.

Pedro Padilla, the demon of 196th Street, not only took her life, but he forever scarred that of her family, and that of the men and women who attempted to find her.

Tommy Keane and Bobby O'Reilly never spoke of this case once it was over and Padilla was convicted. They packed it away like the memories of so many other victims. But it would forever haunt them that they were in the building minutes after she had gone missing, and that she was very possibly, if not very probably, still alive while they were searching for her, while they knocked on the door of the very apartment she died in.

Of course, they had no way of knowing where she was, and it would have been illegal to kick in every door to every apartment in the building, so what were they to do but investigate, search, and ask questions?

Rarely does doing the right thing bring any sort of closure or solace in a case like this. And so for both Tommy Keane and Bobby O'Reilly, the ghost of sweet little Mariana Castro will forever haunt the attics and dark places of their souls.

Hayden Jon Marshall

Chapter One

Tommy opened his eyes to the complete darkness that was the bedroom in his mother's apartment. He reached for his cell phone on the nightstand and saw it was two minutes until the alarm was to go off. Rather than muting it, as he normally would have, he waited for it to sound this morning.

His daughter, Caitlin, had just taught him how to program songs into his phone, and today he would wait for The Clash to start his day with "Train In Vain." Not just because The Clash was one of his favorite bands, and certainly in his top five favorites of all time, but more because he loved that his daughter had taught him something new. Plus, "Train In Vain" was his ex-wife, Cookie's, favorite song by The Clash.

The song began, and Tommy rolled out of bed and onto the floor for his 50 morning pushups. Then he got up and began his morning routine, dressing and preparing for the day, as his mother called to him from the living room.

"Morning, Tommy. Tommy, can I fix you some breakfast, Tommy? Would you like some oatmeal or maybe some eggs, Tommy?"

As he tied his shoes he shouted back, "No thanks, Ma, I'll be fine. I'll…" he paused and thought to himself, 'Have some oatmeal you jerk, why not? The old girl will love fixing it for you, and you can visit for a bit before you head out.'

"You know what, Ma? Oatmeal sounds good, make me a little oatmeal, please," he shouted out to his mother.

"Okay, Tommy, and I'll make it just like you like it, Tommy, with raisins, and walnuts. Tommy, I know you like it like that, Tommy, with some brown sugar, too. But you can do that yourself? I don't want to put too much sugar in it, Tommy," she replied.

"Thanks, Ma. I appreciate it," he shouted back.

They sat at the wooden dining table for the eight to ten minutes it took for Tommy to eat his breakfast. His mother prattled on about her concerns with the President, and what he was or wasn't going to do about Isis, and how they needed to let the generals do their jobs and asked why there weren't real men leading this country anymore.

Maria Keane was an armchair political commentator who avidly watched and read the news. She was quite in tune with current events and was quick to share her opinions on everything from world conflicts to commodity prices.

Tommy humored her as she went on, and thought to himself again, 'This woman doesn't have Alzheimer's. She's far too sharp for that. She's definitely a little crazy, and maybe getting crazier, but she's not losing her memory or functionality... Get her back in to the doctor. Remember to make an appointment soon.' Then he stood and kissed his mother goodbye, and headed out to start his day.

"See you later, Ma. I love you."

"I love you too, Tommy, you be careful today, Tommy. Don't take any chances, Tommy and drive safely please, Tommy."

"Yes, ma'am. I'll see you later."

Tommy left the apartment, took the stairs down, and stepped out onto the building's stoop. He scanned the block from left to right and then left again. It was a fairly warm morning for mid-November as Tommy stepped down the front steps of the stoop and stuffed the keys into his pocket. A young, attractive woman of about 25 stepped out of the vestibule from behind him.

"Hi, Tommy. How are you?" she asked.

Tommy stopped, slightly startled. He turned and stared for a second, not sure who was addressing him. The woman stood about five foot two inches, had shoulder-length, jet black hair, and very large light brown eyes. She was dressed in a tight, black denim jacket, a red hoodie, tight, black skinny jeans and red Converse All-Star sneakers. She looked like she just stepped off the set of an alternative rock video.

"Roya? Is that you? My god, you're all grown up. Shit, I haven't seen you in years. Look at you! You're so big, and so…well, so beautiful. Last time I remember seeing you, you were what, maybe sixteen, seventeen years old?"

Roya smiled, embarrassed by his compliments.

"Yeah, maybe… I don't know, but it's definitely been awhile," she replied.

"How's your mother? I saw her a couple weeks ago, heading into the building, but by the time I got to the door she was already in and up the stairs."

Roya shrugged, "She's my Mom, you know…she has her ways."

Tommy smiled. Roya's mother was an exceptionally unfriendly and bitter woman.

"Ahhh go easy. She's not a bad lady, she maybe just loves you too much," Tommy said. It was an obvious attempt to cover for a woman no one could stand the company of, not even her own young daughter.

"Yeah, well, she is who she is. There's no changing that."

"And you, what are you doing with yourself? You in school?" Tommy asked.

"No, no I graduated from Hunter. I'm working as a computer tech for an investment company. It's a decent job with good pay, but it's so very boring. I'm saving, though, and thinking about grad school, or I don't know, starting something up myself."

"Wow, out of school and working already. Man the time goes fast."

"How's Caitlin?" she asked, "I haven't seen her in years."

Tommy went on to tell Roya all about Caitlin, and how well she was doing as a freshman in the pre-med program up in Sienna, and how proud he was of her.

"Yeah, she's a good kid. I got lucky with that one, never any trouble out of her," he said proudly.

"Yeah, she's a sweetheart," Roya agreed.

"Thanks, well we did what we could. Are you off to work? And can you dress like that at an investment firm?"

Roya laughed, "Yes, actually I'm off to work now and we can wear whatever we like, as techs. No one bothers us. Actually, I'm already running late to meet my friend. I'm walking up to Second Avenue. You going that way?"

"Yes, I am," Tommy replied, and they walked the block up to Second Avenue, reminiscing a bit about their shared past.

"I'd love to catch up sometime though, Tommy. I'm still living upstairs on the fourth floor with my mom, if you'd like to get together one day."

"I'd love that, and really good to see you, Roya. Say hello to your mother for me, please."

"Absolutely," she replied as they reached the corner and went their separate ways.

***

Roya Sarhadi lived her entire life in the same building as Tommy and his mother, in a small two bedroom apartment on the fourth floor. Her parents, Bita and Kourosh, were Persian and came to the United States in the mid-eighties, a few years after the Shah was overthrown in Iran.

Bita's husband, Kourosh, who had emigrated with her, was a chemist, as was Bita Sarhadi. Both were exceptionally intelligent and talented people who fled Iran as the increasing pressure of the new regime restricted their freedoms, and the political climate became too dangerous for intellectuals and free thinkers. Bita and Kourosh, as so many others did, left their country and came to New York in search of a better life, which they had found. Roya, their only child, was born in 1992 in Lenox Hill Hospital. About a year after her birth, her father took a trip back to Iran, for his mother's funeral. It was during this trip that he disappeared. No one knows what happened to Kourosh Sarhadi. His family members said he made it to the funeral and, after the services, returned to his hotel, never to be seen or heard from again.

Roya's mother, Bita, was a very attractive, rather regal looking woman. In her youth she loved British pop music and British culture. Bita and her husband, Kourosh, dressed fashionably in western attire, traveled regularly, and had a good life and a good future in Iran, before the revolution.

Things seemed as though they would be fine in New York. There were many Persian transplants in New York City, and decent jobs available. But unfortunately, Bita Sarhadi was never able to come to terms with her husband's disappearance. She blamed the Iranian government, as part of the great revolution and the persecution that followed. She also blamed the United States government for not doing anything to help her search for her husband. As the years went on and all hope was lost, Bita Sarhadi settled into a life of despair, loneliness, and hatred. This hatred of the world grew so large that it even overshadowed the love she had for her own daughter, Roya, who by all accounts was a perfect little girl. In many ways Roya not only lost her father in 1993, but emotionally lost her mother as well.

The pleasure of seeing Roya for those few minutes, and their brief conversation, made Tommy's morning. He smiled to himself during his walk to the precinct, happy to have run into this young woman he had known for her entire life, and happy to see she had grown into a fine young woman who was working and taking care of herself. He looked forward to telling his ex-wife, Cookie, and daughter, Caitlin, about their meeting.

Tommy continued his walk to the precinct, as he usually did whenever he stayed at his mother's apartment on 88th Street, which was turning out to be most of the time now, since his transfer from the Bronx some seven weeks prior. He enjoyed the convenience of being so close, he also liked seeing his mother daily, although he worked a lot of hours. When he was still assigned to the 5-3 squad in the Bronx, he often worried about his mother. He didn't like her living on her own as she did. He knew there was no way to ever get her to leave that apartment or change her lifestyle though. He also realized that part of his worries for his mother were his own creation. He had ideas about her life and happiness that he assigned to her, and if she had no complaints, well maybe he shouldn't worry at all about the old girl.

***

Tommy arrived at the station house about 20 minutes before his shift, which was typical for him. Tommy was never late and always early. He had no patience for lateness; he hated it in others and would not tolerate it in himself, a trait he most likely picked up during his time in the Army.

Tommy headed up to the Detectives Unit on the second floor. The room was cramped with desks covered in case folders, and the cage, or cell, which currently stood empty, faced the unpopulated squad room. He still did not have a desk of his own so he sat at Doreen Doyle's desk and started to look through some of his open case files that were beginning to pile up. During the Sister Margaret investigation, very little else had gotten any attention, but having a serious homicide to contend with doesn't stop other crimes from happening. Cases do not go away until they are solved, so it was time for Tommy to hunker down to do some serious catch up, and try and get rid of the workload that had accumulated.

As he separated the cases by priority and ease, Detective Doreen Doyle walked into the squad room, followed by Sergeant Browne.

"Good morning, good morning," Tommy said to them both as they entered.

"What's shakin' bacon?" Doyle replied, flashing a broad smile at Tommy.

"Good morning, Tom," said Sergeant Browne, "It's just the three of us today. Stein has court, Colletti banged in, he had something going on with his car he had to take care of, and Lieutenant Bricks is on vacation this week. So do whatever needs doing and let's see if you can get rid of some of your older cases before COMPSTAT time."

COMPSTAT was the weekly meeting held at One Police Plaza, where crime statistics were compared and strategies to combat them decided upon. It was the most important day of the week for people like Captain Peleggi. But it was of no interest at all to a squad detective like Tommy, who's only concern was solving crimes and catching criminals on behalf of the victims of the City of New York.

"You got it, boss. I got a pile of shit adding up here I need to get rid of," Tommy replied, as he continued to make notes on his folders and in his notepad. He then stood and moved his files and notes over to Stein's desk.

"Here you go, Doreen, sit." He motioned for her to sit at her own desk.

"Thanks, Tommy, that's not necessary though. I've got plenty of room here, especially with everyone out of the office today," she replied.

"Yeah, but this is your desk, Doreen, and you should be sitting at it."

"Well, thank you sir, I appreciate that. What do you have going today, Tommy? I have a couple of interviews I'd like to do and hope to get this husband to come in later for a domestic -- hopefully just give him a desk appearance ticket. I don't think I'll need to put him through the system... Do you have anything pressing?" Doreen asked.

"Not anything pressing. The pressing issue is, I have too much open bullshit here. A few interviews, and maybe a collar or two, and I should be able to close most of these this week, I think. But it's just a pile of shit I need to clean off my desk right now. Let me type up a few of these reports and we'll head out for some interviews and follow ups for the both of us, cool?"

"Perfection. I'm in the same boat -- all simple stuff right now. I just need to get it all done and gone."

They both continued to work on their caseloads, made notes and phone calls, for approximately an hour.

Finally, Tommy dropped his pen down on the battered desk and leaned back in his chair.

"You about ready to head out, Doreen?" He asked, "I need to stop by this grand larceny over on Park Avenue for an interview. Complaint says this woman had a pair of earrings stolen, and the complainant says they're worth a hundred and twenty thousand dollars. Can you believe that? A hundred and twenty thousand dollars for a pair of earrings? I don't care how much money you have, a hundred and twenty thousand dollars is a disgusting amount of money to spend on earrings." Tommy shook his head slowly.

"Oh God, do I agree with you there, Tommy. Some of these people spend their money on the inanest things. All the problems there are in the world, and they'll spend more than my apartment cost me, on a piece of jewelry. Something that literally means nothing in the real world. Anyway yeah, let's get out of here, I can't sit in the office all day; the heat is killing me in here," Doreen replied. Pushing her strawberry blond hair back off her face, she momentarily exposed the scarring on her neck from the hot oil attack she had endured years before, when she was assigned to the Housing Unit in Brooklyn.

"I know, it's fuckin' project hot in here today."

"Project hot," Doreen Doyle smiled, making her green eyes sparkle, "You're too funny, Tommy."

"I'm funny? You came from Housing, Doreen, you know exactly what I'm talking about."

"Yeah, I do. Man those buildings were like ovens sometimes. Funny though…well not ha ha funny… either they were boiling hot or there was no heat at all and the tenants had to keep the ovens on with the doors open just to get a little warmth," she replied. Then she shouted loud enough for Sergeant Browne to hear, "Tommy and I are heading out, Sarge. Got some interviews to do."

"Copy that!" Sergeant Browne replied from his office.

"You hungry, Doreen, or you wanna just head straight over to my Park Avenue complaint?" Tommy asked as they headed out of the squad room and down the stairs.

"No, I'm good, Tommy. Let's get started and break for meal around eleven or twelve. I had a bagel and a coffee on the way in," Doreen replied.

"Very good, I'm in the same boat. Had me a little oatmeal this morning along with the morning news report."

"Anything new on the news this morning?"

"Nah, the reporter pretty much reported the same as she does every other day... Isis is running amuck and we have no real men running the country anymore."

"Ha, ain't that the truth," Doreen replied. "So let me ask you, Tommy. What is a real man to you? You're a pretty manly man I think. What's a real man in your eyes?" Doreen asked inquisitively, and paused on the steps outside the precinct, hoping for an interesting answer.

"A real man? Well, Doreen, a real man isn't a guy who rides a motorcycle or falls out of an airplane with a parachute on his back, or chases bad guys around the streets of some city, risking his life in defense of some idea of law and order, or bangs three strippers from Scores one night and manages to satisfy all their feminine desires... No, I think, well in my opinion anyway, a real man is a guy who gets up every day and goes to work -- usually to a job he hates -- so he can properly take care of his family. A real man loves and respects his wife and kids and sacrifices his own wants and desires to help, well, maybe help them have a decent life, and hopefully a better life than the one he himself has had."

"Wow... good answer there, Mr. Man. You know, I really like how you think, Tommy," Doreen replied with a satisfied smile.

"Yeah, well, I had a good breakfast this morning, maybe that's helping me think a little better and wax poetic today?"

***

09:46 AM - 937 Park Avenue

Tommy and Doreen parked their Crown Vic and walked up to the complainant's home, at 937 Park Avenue, to inquire about the earring theft. The building was pale cream stone and deep reddish brown Klinker brick, with a hunter green awning. Short, black, wrought iron planters containing well-manicured shrubs and ivy, were situated just outside of the entrance.

The doorman of the building -- a young, tall, good-looking man, with a bored to death look on his face, dressed in an all grey, wool serge uniform and hat with white gloves -- opened the wrought iron door. He asked, in a sullen tone that matched the expression on his face, "Good morning, who are you here to see, and who may I ask is calling, please?"

"Hey, how you doing pal? Detectives Keane and Doyle here to see a Mrs. Gillstone in apartment 7A," Tommy replied.

He pulled back his coat to reveal the Detective shield clipped on his belt.

"Okay, Officers, I'll have to ask you to go around the corner, please, and go through the service entrance. The handyman on duty will take you up in the service elevator," the doorman explained.

Tommy looked at him for a couple of seconds, "What? Excuse me? You want us to do what?"

"I'm sorry, sir, you have to use the service entrance. The main elevator is for residents and their guests only."

Tommy took an extra step closer to the doorman and stared at him with his cold, deadpan eyes.

"Listen. We may be here to protect and to serve, but we ain't nobody's fucking servants. We're not delivering furniture, or a pizza, and we're certainly not anyone's paid help. Now get this. This Mrs. Gillstone made a complaint, and we are here to interview her and begin an investigation of said complaint, and if you, or her, or anyone else thinks we're going to go around the corner and use the service elevator, you're dead fucking wrong. Now, hit her bell, announce us, and tell her we're on our way up...You got that?"

"Hey, I'm just telling you the rules, man. Believe me, I don't make any of these policies. I just gotta do what I'm told."

"Okay. I know, and I get it pal. I'm sorry, I'm not looking to give you a hard time, just tell her we're on our way up, please."

"Yes, sir." The door man pushed the corresponding button on the brass panel on the wall and lifted the handset, announcing that the police were on their way up.

Tommy and Doreen walked from the front vestibule into the green marbled hallway. They passed two gold-colored wing chairs and matching settee, and headed towards the elevator straight ahead.

"Ha. Good job, Tommy," Doreen said in a low voice, bumping his arm with her shoulder.

Sitting on a stool inside the elevator was an elevator operator -- a short, round man, with squinty eyes and rosy cheeks. It was the complexion of a man who has a pint of gin, or possibly some blackberry brandy, in his locker that helps his coffee taste just right and gets him through eight or more hours a day of continuously riding an elevator up and down. Day in and day out, month after month, for twenty plus years. This seemingly more jolly employee of the building smiled brightly as Tommy and Doreen approached the elevator. Dressed in the same grey uniform and white gloves as the doorman, he bowed his head to both detectives as they stepped into the over-the-top brass and green marble box.

"Good morning. What floor are you visiting today, please?"

"Seven, my good man," Tommy replied.

"Yes, sir." The elevator operator pushed the button for the seventh floor.

"Look at this!" Tommy exclaimed to Doreen, "These rich fuckers in this building can't even push a button in the elevator themselves. How lazy and privileged can someone be?"

"Shhh, Tommy, let's not get any complaints today, okay?"

"You two on the Job?" The elevator man asked.

"Yes, sir, we are... Does it show?" Doreen replied.

"It shows. Who you going to see, 7A or 7B?"

"That's our choices? there's only two apartments per floor? Wow, they must be nice apartments... A, we're going to 7A," Tommy answered.

"Gillstone," the elevator man said, with a bit of contempt, "Woman's a trip. Young, trust fund kid, 'bout 35, married to Jarred Gillstone, 'bout 55, fuckin' loaded. He's rarely home, in China now, buying or selling some businesses. That's what he does, buys businesses, fires everyone, then sells 'em off to foreign countries. And the wife, Erica, she's a nervous wreck, busy-body, up everyone's ass all the time 'bout the most unimportant things. They keep their two kids locked up in some fancy boarding school in Connecticut. Costs more each year than all three of our salaries combined. Let me tell you something, these people may have money, but they got no class."

"Thanks for the insight pal. We appreciate it," Tommy replied.

"No problem, my brother's on the job, works in the 6-6 in Brooklyn. Tommy, Tommy Espana, same last name as me. Either of you know him?"

"No, I don't know that name," Tommy said.

"No, me neither," Doreen replied, "I worked in Brooklyn, but was in Housing."

"Housing... Ha, well you're moving on up today, sister." The elevator man laughed. "Yeah I woulda liked to have been a cop too, but I took a pinch back in the 80's. Got caught buying a little nose candy one night in the 7-5 before a night of clubbing, and that was it for me. Young and stupid, and here I am now doing the doorman thing for the last 28 years."

"I'm sorry, pal. Yeah there's no forgiveness on this job for drug use. It ain't the Fire Department. How they treating you here?" Tommy replied.

"Not a bad gig. You know. It's got its ups and downs," Mr. Espana said with a smirk as the door opened to the 7th Floor. "The door on the left... and good luck with this one... The woman's a trip."

Tommy and Doreen exited the elevator and stood in front of the door marked A. Tommy knocked lightly, and a young, Central American woman in a blue uniform answered the door.

"Hello, you are the police, yes? Here to see Mrs. Gillstone, yes?"

"Yes, and yes," Tommy replied.

"Please, please come in, please. Please wait here one moment, please."

She left Tommy and Doreen standing on the burgundy marbled floor in the entranceway of the apartment. Tommy eyed the foyer and took in the painting hanging on the pure white wall, over a small table that held a huge bouquet of fresh flowers. The painting was abstract and muddled with bright colors. 'Money doesn't buy taste,' Tommy thought to himself. A minute or two passed before the detectives could hear her high-heeled shoes quickly click clack their way towards them on the marble floors from a distant room. Mrs. Erica Gillstone entered the foyer, from one of the side corridors.

Mrs. Gillstone, a thin and attractive woman, appeared wearing well fitted black pants and a royal blue silk blouse, with black pumps that had matching royal blue soles. Her look was that of wealth and perfection, although she did seem rather overdressed, or maybe just too magazine-shoot-ready for ten in the morning.

"Detectives. How are you this morning? And what took you so long to get here? The police took my complaint yesterday afternoon. I had expected you to arrive sometime yesterday, after they left." This is how she greeted them, as she approached with a black binder in her hand.

"Sorry, Mrs. Gillstone, we got here as soon as we could," Tommy replied.

"Well, this is a very serious matter, Detective. I'm sorry, what is your name, Detective?"

"Keane, ma'am, Detective Keane."

"Ahh, Detective Keane. Well Detective, this is a very serious matter. You see, a pair of very, very valuable, very expensive, and very sentimental earrings have been stolen from me by one of my house staff, here in the apartment."

Tommy opened his notebook and began taking notes.

"Okay, so how much were these earrings worth, ma'am?"

"At least one hundred and twenty thousand dollars."

"Okay… And you say you know who took them?"

"Yes, Marta. Marta who was one of our house staff, here in the apartment. She was fairly new, she'd only been with us for about nine months. She's definitely the one who stole my earrings."

"Okay… Definitely the one, huh? How do you know she was the one? Did you see her take them? Do you have her on video, or something? Did someone tell you she took them? How, may I ask, do you know Marta ran off with your earrings, Mrs. Gillstone?"

"Well, I know because she is the only one who would, the only one who would do such a thing. She's young, and brash, and sneaky." Mrs. Gillstone lifted her chin slightly, in defiance.

"Okay. Other than brash and sneaky, what can you tell me about Miss Marta, the maid?"

"Well, for starters, she lives in the Bronx. I have her address and phone number within the file I have compiled for you. She is from Costa Rica, she lives with her sister and her sister's husband, up there in the Bronx. She is very sneaky, always acting suspicious when she is doing her work around the house here."

"Okay. And what exactly did Marta do for you, Mrs. Gillstone?"

"She cleaned, did laundry, made the beds, ran errands when needed. You know, typical staff things."

"No, actually, I don't know. That's why I'm asking, Mrs. Gillstone. Now, you say you know Marta ran off with your earrings. But other than you knowing this, do you have any physical proof that it was indeed Marta who stole your earrings, Mrs. Gillstone?"

"Well… no, nothing physical. But I know it was her. Isn't that enough for you?"

"Well… no, not exactly, ma'am. Do you have a photograph, or maybe a receipt, for these earrings? Something we can go on, so we know what we are looking for?"

"Yes, in the file you will find a photo, and also will see them on the list of insured valuables." She handed Tommy the black binder she had been holding.

As Tommy's inquiry went on, Doreen, who was standing just behind him, heard a radio call:

"2-1 Squad, 2-1 Squad, Patrol requesting 85 forthwith at John Jay Park for missing child."

"2-1 Squad central. Copy, en route to location," was Doreen's response.

"Excuse me, Tommy," Doreen interrupted, "We have a missing child at John Jay Park and patrol is requesting us to 85 them there forthwith."

"Tell them we're on our way," Tommy replied, snapping his notebook closed. "Mrs. Gillstone, we will be in touch. Thank you so much for the file, I'm sure this will help us out tremendously."

"Wait… what? Where are you going? This is a very, very important case, Detective."

"Yes, ma'am, it sure is. But right now we have a missing child that we need to attend to, Mrs. Gillstone, and your earrings are just going to have to wait. You will hear from me soon, Mrs. Gillstone, but we have to leave right now."

"Are you kidding me, Detective?" She raised her voice, as Tommy and Doreen exited the apartment door and pushed the button for the elevator.

"Detectives!" She shouted again as they got on the elevator.

"Told you. That woman's a trip," Mr. España, the elevator operator, said once the doors closed.

Chapter Two

10:18 AM - John Jay Park

Keane and Doyle arrived at the entrance to John Jay Park, on Cherokee Place. It was a park Tommy was very familiar with. Oftentimes as a teenager, during the hot New York City summers, he and his friends would make the walk down to John Jay park and climb -- or cut a hole in -- the fence, to go swimming in the two pools after the park was closed. Then years later, John Jay Park was one of the places he would occasionally bring his daughter Caitlin, when they still lived on East 81st Street.

Upon arrival, they were approached by Officer Rios, a young, handsome officer of about five foot seven, with a thin mustache and a determined look on his face. Rios was one of two uniformed patrol officers who responded to the scene. The three of them stood at the threshold of the park, next to the brick columns and the tall, black, wrought iron fence. Looking in, they could see the playground, with the pool house to the left, the East River straight ahead, and the basketball and handball courts to the right.

"Morning, Detectives. We have a missing three year old. The mother is over here," Officer Rios said, pointing toward the benches to the left of the entrance, with his radio in his hand. "Mrs. Marshall. She was sitting on the bench over there as her kid played, and she said she looked up from her laptop and he just wasn't there anymore. We put out a description over the radio and everyone is looking for him. Here, I wrote it down for you." Officer Rios handed Tommy the child's description. "Sergeant Webber is on his way also, so as far as I know, a mobilization hasn't been called yet and no Amber Alert put out either," Rios explained to both Keane and Doyle, as they scanned the surroundings.

"Very good. Thanks, Rios. Has anyone left the park since you arrived?" Tommy asked.

"No. No one's really here. We got here just maybe ten, twelve minutes ago, if that. Just the few people you see now is who was here. This is the only way in and out, and so far, no one has passed us." Rios opened his memo book and read off the child's description to him, "He's a white male, three years old, brown hair, grey bubble jacket, navy blue pants, grey and blue knit hat, and he was carrying, or last seen with, a brown stuffed bunny."

Tommy's eyes continued to scan the park as he replied.

"Great, thanks. Do me a favor, Rios, don't let anyone leave, okay? We're gonna want to talk to everyone here. Hopefully this won't take too long," Tommy said.

Tommy and Doreen approached the visibly shaken woman who sat on the bench, near some concrete camels in the playground, where Officer Rios had asked her to wait.

"Hello Miss. I'm Detective Keane, and this is my partner, Detective Doyle, from the 21st Precinct. I understand you've lost your three year-old son?"

The woman was small and thin, and approximately thirty-five years of age. She was dressed well, wearing a black down coat with a fur collar, denim jeans, and what appeared to be expensive tan suede boots.

"Yes. Yes, hello," she said through tears as she looked up at the detectives. "My name, my name is Jessica Marshall." Her voice cracked and got higher as she continued in a more panicked voice, "and I can't find my son! My son, Hayden, my son Hayden... He's only three... Oh my god, oh my god, Hayden!" she cried out as she rose to her feet. "He's only three!" she repeated, her entire body shaking in uncontrollable fear.

Another woman, approximately the same age as Mrs. Marshall, stepped forward from the side. She was short, with light brown, very wavy hair, and wearing a brown cable-knit sweater, with a navy down vest over it, denim jeans and sneakers. She was holding hands with a young girl about four years old.

"Hello, Detectives. I called 911 when she noticed her son was missing. My daughter and I were playing in the swings, over there, and I noticed her panicking and starting to shout for her son. We began to look everywhere for him and when we couldn't find him, I called 911."

"Doreen, can you calm Ms. Marshall, while I speak with Ms. ..."

"Brownstein," the woman answered.

"Brownstein," Tommy said as he turned toward the other woman and walked a few feet away. Doreen gently took

Mrs. Marshall's arm, and seated her back on the bench, then sat down next to her.

"What can you tell us, Ms. Brownstein?"

"Nothing really," she replied. "I was at the swings with my daughter, and I noticed this woman looking around frantically, and calling for her son again and again. I pulled my daughter out of the swings and went over and asked her what was wrong. She, she said that she lost her son and I began to help her look. We both called for him, over and over, and we searched the entire park. And then I called 911, and in maybe two minutes those officers arrived and then you detectives came walking into the park. Really, that's about it."

"Do you know this woman? Do you know Ms. Marshall at all?"

"No, I've never seen her before," she replied, shaking her head.

"Did you notice anything unusual about her boy?" Tommy asked, and Ms. Brownstein knitted her brows.

"Actually… no… well, I didn't see him at all actually. I was just playing with my daughter, when I saw her panic, and asked to help."

"So you didn't see her son?"

"No… No, sir, I didn't."

"Okay. Can I ask you to wait a bit in case we have any further questions?"

"Of course, no problem," she replied.

Tommy then went to speak to a tall, older white male, who appeared to be in his 70's. He was standing with Rios at the entrance, wearing a long grey herringbone coat with a matching grey Scally Cap and holding a black wooden cane.

"Hello, sir, I'm Detective Keane from the 21st Precinct. This woman here has lost her son. Did you notice anything unusual, or see the boy at all?"

"I didn't see the boy when I came in a while ago, I noticed the mother over there on the bench, by the camels, typing away at her laptop computer. But no, I didn't see, or take notice, of her boy at the time."

"Notice anything that was unusual to you in the park today? Anything at all, no matter how small it may seem?"

"No, sir, Detective. It's a quiet day today. A nice day, pretty warm for November, I think. But it feels as though it's getting colder already. No one really here -- that woman and her son, the other one over there with her daughter. There was an African nanny here, a while ago, with two little ones but she left when I was walking in. Nothing unusual, no suspicious characters, no sir."

"How long have you been here, sir?"

"Oh, I don't know, maybe 40, 50 minutes. I walked in and sat over there, near the FDR, and watched a couple of tug boats pulling some barges up the river for a bit. Came to life and started to look for that boy, when his mother and the other nice lady were searching and shouting for him."

"Thank you, sir. Please wait a bit, in case we have any further questions."

"Of course, of course, anything to help," the old man replied.

Tommy turned and shouted over to Rios, who had stepped back towards the park entrance.

"Rios, you have his info?"

"Yes, sir," Officer Rios replied.

Returning back to Ms. Brownstein, Tommy asked, "Where did you look, Ms. Brownstein?"

"Everywhere in the park here, and then we went up to the avenue as well."

"York Avenue?"

"Yes, that's where I called from. And then I asked this woman… the mother, to come back to the park, while we waited for you… the police."

"Good… good. You did the right thing. Thank you," Tommy told her and then got on the radio.

"2-1 Squad central, we have a missing male child, three years of age, last seen in a grey bubble jacket, navy pants, and grey and blue hat, with a brown toy stuffed rabbit, in the vicinity of John Jay Park, 7-7 Street off York Avenue. Please notify all units, and have any available units, and aviation, assist in an area search, please."

"10-4, 2-1 Squad."

Tommy's heart suddenly started pounding faster. A sense of panic and urgency came over him. The thought, and the fear, that they weren't going to find this child right away, slipped into his mind. 'Where is this boy? Where could he possibly be? How did he just disappear from the park like that, and how did his mother not notice him walk off, or get snatched?' The questions filled his mind in seconds, blurring his thoughts and concentration. Tommy regained his train of thought as he heard the police helicopter slowly move overhead, no doubt looking for young Hayden from above.

He walked over to the bench where Doyle and Jessica Marshall sat.

"Are you married, Ms. Marshall?" Tommy asked.

"Yes, her husband, David Marshall, is on his way right now," Doreen answered for her.

'So, this won't be an ex-husband-estranged father kidnapping situation,' he thought to himself, almost hoping that would be the answer and that they would not only have a lead, but that the child may be safer somehow.

"Listen, Mrs. Marshall, we're going to find your son. We have uniformed officers looking all over the area. And did you notice that helicopter slowly go by overhead? They are also looking for Hayden right now -- they're checking all the rooftops, and alleyways, everywhere we can't see from down here on street level. We'll find him, I promise."

It was a promise Tommy could only hope to keep, but an assurance he felt he had to give to Mrs. Marshall. Tommy's heart started pounding again, 'God I hope we find this kid,' he thought, knowing all too well, that it may not be the case.

"What did you do?!" A voice shouted from behind Tommy's back. "What did you do, you stupid bitch?! Where is he? What did you do? How, how? How could you be so stupid, you fucking asshole, where is he? Where is my son? What did you do to our son?" Jessica Marshall's husband, David Marshall, screamed like a mad man, as he rushed into John Jay Park, past Tommy, straight towards his crying wife.

David Marshall stood about five-foot-eight. He wore a brown knit cap, with reddish-orange geometric designs knitted into it, and ear flaps dangling down the sides of his half-bearded face. His jacket was a short, black down parka with yellow trim, and had about ten different ski lift passes hanging from the zipper. Underneath, he wore a brown and grey Pendleton flannel shirt, which was untucked and fell over the top of his tan corduroy pants. His skin was flushed red, as he furrowed his brow in anger beneath his black and orange framed glasses.

As David approached his wife like a man possessed, Doreen stood up from the bench and stood in front of Jessica, getting in between them. Tommy reached out and physically stopped him with a hand to his chest, as David Marshall stepped a little too close to both Doreen and his wife.

"Slow down, Mr. Marshall," Tommy commanded, in a strong tone. David Marshall slapped at Tommy's hand.

"Take your hands off me! Don't touch me, do not ever touch me," the man cried out, as he tried to move around Tommy to get to his wife. "Where is my son?... Jessica! What have you done?"

"Relax, Mr. Marshall, we're looking for him now," Tommy began.

"Relax? Who are you, the Police? Well, what are you doing here? Why aren't you looking for him somewhere else? It's obvious he isn't here. Isn't it obvious to you he isn't here,

Officer?" David Marshall screamed as he took a step back from Tommy's outstretched arm.

"We have people looking all over the area for your boy, Mr. Marshall. We have helicopters in the sky, and officers everywhere with his description. Now please, sir, relax. We need to ask you some questions."

"Relax? Relax? And what do you need to ask me? He was with that stupid bitch, on the bench over there, she, her, that stupid bitch, she was the one he was with, not me. She's the one who lost him. Did she tell you anything? Does she know what happened? I bet she knows nothing, does she? I bet the spoiled, princess bitch knows nothing. Do You, Bitch?" David Marshall screamed, his face a violent red, as spittle formed at the corners of his mouth. He tried again to move around Tommy, but Tommy stepped forward, and to the side, and stared into Mr. Marshall's face.

"Alright! Enough with the fucking cursing, you. You're gonna relax now, and we're going to ask you some questions. Do you understand me, Mr. Marshall?" Tommy asked, flatly and firmly.

David Marshall looked into Tommy's eyes with a fire of rage, but once meeting Tommy's cold, dead stare, he became speechless. The flame of rage was extinguished, as fear and helplessness took over. His eyes went straight to the pavement below and his posture deflated.

"Yes, sir. Yes, Detective. Of course, of course, forgive me," he said in a low, monotone voice. "I'm sorry; I know my outburst was of no help."

"Alright, it's alright. We understand, Mr. Marshall. This is a very stressful situation. We have several questions to ask you and Mrs. Marshall. Do you live nearby? Can we take you home and talk to you there? It seems to be getting colder out. Besides, I'm sure Mrs. Marshall would like to leave the stress of the park here, for a little privacy for our interview, and to warm up."

"Yeah, uh, sure. We live just up the avenue, on 79th Street." David Marshall replied, rather sheepishly.

"Okay, we'll head over there then. Please just give me a minute."

Tommy stepped aside and put a call into Sergeant Browne.

"Hey Sarge, how you doing? Tommy here, Can you help us out and have an Amber Alert put out for a white male, three years old. Name is Hayden Marshall, wearing a grey bubble jacket, navy pants, grey and blue knit cap, and carrying a brown stuffed toy rabbit."

"Oh, Christ. Yeah, Tommy, I'll get that right out. Good luck," Sergeant Browne replied.

"Thanks, Boss."

***

Detective Keane and Detective Doyle walked Mr. and Mrs. Marshall back to their building at 453 East 79th Street. There they had a small two-bedroom apartment on the ninth floor of an older brick high rise. They silently entered the building, and both Mr. Marshall and Tommy nodded to the doorman, as Doreen guided Mrs. Marshall in. Jessica stared at the floor, in a mild state of shock, as they walked on the black carpet runners that were laid out across the dark red terrazzo floors from the entrance to the elevator. The elevator ride was silent.

The four of them entered the apartment and Tommy immediately started taking mental notes. He had wanted to see where they lived, which is why he suggested the apartment and not the precinct for the interview. Not only would the couple, hopefully, feel more comfortable at home but it would enable Tommy to see not just where they lived, but how they lived. It was another glimpse into their lives and it may enable him to note if there were any signs of neglect, abuse, or any other clues that may change the path of the investigation.

The four sat in the living area, on a chrome and leather sofa set, that was obviously expensive, but not the least bit comfortable. Tommy had a jolt of a memory, looking at the leather living room set, of another missing persons case that hadn't ended well, and he quickly pushed it away.

Jessica curled up in the corner of the couch, trying to get as physically and emotionally far from her husband as she could. Tommy and Doreen began by asking them simple questions about Hayden. They wanted to know his weight, size, and clothing description from his jacket, to what socks and underwear he wore that day. Tommy gave them his cell phone number and asked them to send some photos to him. They asked if there was anything unusual about Hayden. Was he shy, outgoing, hyper, or autistic? Had he ever wandered off before? Was there anyone in the world they would suspect that would want to take Hayden, or hurt their family, in any way?

No answer gave any glimpse of wrongdoing, other than the fact that Jessica Marshall simply had not been paying attention to her son while he played in the park. And on more than one occasion, David Marshall brought that up, in between questions.

"What were you doing, Jessica, shopping on your phone? Who were you texting that you didn't see him disappear, Jessica? Your mother? Or maybe your trainer, Jeremy?"

Tommy scanned the apartment carefully, but the place was neat and clean. He didn't care for the décor, but there was no crime in having minimalist tastes, uncomfortable furniture, and abstract art on the walls.

"May I see Hayden's room, please?" Tommy asked.

"Of course, Detective," David Marshall replied. He stood and led him to the room just off the living area. 'A pretty stereotypical three-year-old's room,' Tommy thought, seeing nothing unusual. The walls were painted blue, with two large decals of a dolphin and a beluga whale. There was an unmade twin bed with sheets that also had a sea life theme. Stuffed toys were strewn about the room; on the floor, on the bed, and on the nightstand, intermingled with multi-colored building blocks and a couple of large, plastic trucks.

Tommy stepped in and carefully looked around but touched nothing as he saw nothing that piqued his interest. David Marshall followed Tommy into the room and while both were out of sight and earshot of Mrs. Marshall and Detective Doyle, Tommy stepped closer to Mr. Marshall and spoke softly.

"Listen, Mr. Marshall, I know this is a very scary time for you. Please, sir, if I may, please take it easy on your wife." A glint of rage, from earlier, returned to David Marshall's eyes, but he did not lose his composure.

"Yes, Detective, I understand. And I know, I know, it's just so… so unnerving." A tear, and a wince, came to his face. "I'm fucking terrified," he mumbled softly to Tommy.

"I know you are," Tommy replied, "We'll find him, I assure you."

"Please, Detective, he's all I have."

A loud shriek was heard from Jessica Marshall and the two men went quickly back into the living area of the apartment, where Detective Doyle sat with her arm around Jessica Marshall, who was crying loudly on the couch. As Tommy and David entered the room Doreen told them, "The Amber Alert just came over her phone for Hayden."

"Oh god," David Marshall said softly. The Amber Alert was a knockout blow of reality to the couple. Over the years they had seen, and discarded, probably dozens of them, but now it was their son, it was their little Hayden.

Tommy placed his hand on David's shoulder for a moment, letting him know he recognized his pain and his fear, then walked over to Jessica who still sat sobbing into Doreen's shoulder, and placed his hand on her shoulder for a moment, too.

"We'll find him, Mrs. Marshall. I promise, we'll find your son." He removed his hand and then straightened up.

"We're going to leave you now. I think we have enough information, for the moment. Contact us immediately if you think of anything, no matter how small, anything that you believe may be of interest to us. You have my card and my cell number. Please do not hesitate any time of the day or night, if you think of something. Call me."

The Marshalls both thanked the detectives, as they left the apartment.

Tommy and Doreen rode the elevator down and Doreen asked, "What do you think, Tommy?"

"Fuck if I know, Doreen. Right now we have nothing to run with; I see no signs of abuse here in the apartment, and I think both parents seem sincere in their distress & panic. It does strike me odd that no one saw the boy in the park other than Mrs. Marshall though... What are your thoughts? "

"My thoughts are pretty much the same, Tommy. Nothing I could see in the apartment would make me think they didn't care for their son. Everything is neat and clean, I saw toys and photos of him, everything makes me think he was loved, and she, Mrs. Marshall seems genuinely distraught. and David, well, he also seems to be honestly and rightfully upset... But man, he's an intense guy. Do you think she's going to be okay with him?"

"He's scared, terrified, out of his mind with fear, so is she. This is the kind of thing that kills marriages. If we find this boy or not, this is the kind of thing that can rip a family apart."

"You don't think we'll find him?"

"God, I hope so... But do you remember what they told you in the academy about abductions, Doreen?"

"What? 80 Percent?"

"Yup, 80 percent. 80 percent of people who are abducted are dead within the first three hours, and this Hayden boy has now been missing for over one."

"God... I don't even want to think about it."

"Well, it's our job to think about it, kid. Let's see what we can do to find this boy, and let's hope when we do, he's still alive."

Hayden Jon Marshall

Chapter Three

Detectives Keane and Doyle canvassed the blocks surrounding the park. They asked every merchant, in every storefront, if they had seen little Hayden. Every doorman and super they came across, the mailman, the school crossing guard, anyone working within four blocks of the park, was questioned. They collected some video from a few shops that ran along the route between the Marshalls' apartment and John Jay Park. They re-searched the park, although it had been thoroughly gone over by both the detectives, and patrol officers, and still nothing.

The detectives walked into the large building, called the Pavilion, located at 500 East 77th Street -- a massive white brick building that housed 210 apartments. Built in the mid-sixties, it was the height of luxury at the time and still held a reputation as one of the finer post-war apartment buildings in the area.

Upon entering, they were met by a tall Middle Eastern doorman in a dark navy uniform. Tommy and Doreen identified themselves and asked the doorman about the cameras outside, specifically if they viewed the park. The doorman asked them to wait while he walked behind the desk and made a phone call.

"Okay, Detectives, please come this way. Go down this hall here and make a left, then walk down the hall there and there will be a door on the left that says 'Security.' Please go that way and someone will help you."

Both detectives thanked the doorman and when they made the first left they saw a short, attractive woman of about 40, with short dark hair, dressed in a pantsuit, and waiting for them at the end of the hallway.

"Right this way, Detectives. How may I help you today?" the woman asked

"Hello, I'm Detective Keane and this is Detective Doyle from the 21st precinct, and we'd like to know if you have a camera that faces the park?"

"Unfortunately we don't. There are cameras all around the building but they all face down to the sidewalks surrounding the building to see what happens along our perimeter, with the exception of the one that faces out onto 77th Street, where the cars pull into the driveway. That one looks out and across the street."

"May we see what you have, please?" Tommy asked.

"Of course you can, but know I can't give you copies of anything without a subpoena."

"Of course, we understand," Tommy replied.

The woman walked them into the office, and then into another room behind the office, where a young blonde woman sat looking at a large security monitor.

"What would you like to see?" the woman asked.

"If we could see that 77th Street camera from about 9:00 AM through to 10:15 AM, please."

The blonde cued up the video, and the four of them watched it run at four times the normal speed.

"There, right there, Tommy," Doreen said excitedly when she saw Mrs. Marshall walk by.

"Can we rewind that, please?" she asked.

They all watched Mrs. Marshall walk by, but due to the fountain in front of the building and the cars parked on both sides of the street, all they could see was her head, and no sign of little Hayden.

"She's there, but we can't see Hayden," Doreen said out loud.

"Nope, he's too little, his little head doesn't, or wouldn't, make it up over the cars or that fountain from this view. Do you ladies have anything else possibly facing that side of the street or the entrance to the park?"

"No, sir, I'm sorry," the blonde woman replied.

"Well, thank you ladies. Thank you very much for your time. Here is my card, so you know who was here. Thank you so much."

"Sorry, I wish we could help, Detectives. Is this... this is for that little boy that went missing, isn't it? I saw the Amber Alert."

"Yes, ma'am, it is."

"I thought so. Good luck and please, if we can help at all, please return."

"Thank you, we will."

***

On the sidewalk outside of the Pavilion, Doreen began, "I don't like this, Tommy. I find it hard to believe Jessica Marshall had anything to do with her son's disappearance after everything we've seen this morning, but how is it no one has seen them together yet? And now we can't see him on this little bit of video?"

"I was thinking the same thing, Doreen. I don't believe, or at least at this stage think, she is responsible for the boy's disappearance, other than by not paying attention. Her emotions and entire vibe lead me to believe she is innocent of any wrongdoing other than not keeping an eye out... But it's not what we think or feel, it's what we know. And right now, unfortunately, we don't know shit. We'll definitely have to run a background check on her and her husband, and look into them a bit. I don't suspect either of them of any kind of foul play here, but we also can't rule them out. I've seen some cases flip to where the most unsuspected person ends up being the perp in the end, and nothing surprises me anymore."

***

Tommy and Doreen headed back to the precinct to watch the few bits of video, taken from the surrounding buildings and businesses that had security cameras, but once again, nothing. It was as if this three-year-old boy just vanished.

They also ran checks on both Jessica and David Marshall, both of whom came up clean, as far as any past criminal history. All checks on their social media also came back innocuous. Certainly this wasn't going to end further investigations into the couple, but on the surface Tommy and Doreen had nothing on them to even hint at any wrongdoing now, or ever. That, combined with everything they knew about the morning's disappearance of Hayden Jon, had checked out. It was another wall in the investigation.

"So, what now, Tommy?" Doyle asked, as she leaned back in her chair with an exasperated look on her face, "What have we missed, Tommy? What didn't we do?"

"Well, we're doing what we're supposed to be doing, Doreen. There's got to be something here for us, something that leads us to this boy. We'll see if we can enhance some of this surveillance video and check the license plates of any cars that may have driven down the block around that time. Also, we'll run a computer check on anyone in the area who may have any past crimes we need to know about."

"Okay, I'll do that now, before I sign out and see what comes back. Why don't you head home, Tommy? We've been at this for hours and it'll be awhile before we get anything back. I think I'm a little more proficient on the computer than you are, anyway," Doreen said with a smile. "Tomorrow you'll be rested and have a fresh new look at all of this."

"Thanks, Doreen. I think maybe you're right and I think I'll take you up on that. See you in the morning."

"Yes, sir. I'll see you tomorrow, Tommy."

Tommy signed out, left the precinct and walked back to John Jay Park. He, once again, walked through the playground and around the perimeter of the fenced-in park. It was now dark and he didn't know what he might find, but he couldn't just go home and leave this case alone. There was a child missing, and the thought of it was eating at him. A three year-old little boy, where could he be? Who would have taken him?

Tommy finally left the park and began heading home. He was frustrated with the fruitless events of the day and downright scared for the wellbeing of Hayden. His usual calm, meditative approach to his investigations was thrown off at the thought of little Hayden's body lying dead, somewhere in the city, or being held, by who knew who, some deranged pedophile, or any number of crazies, that would steal a three year-old boy.

Was it possible it was the boy's mother? Tommy didn't suspect her for his disappearance, but she was the last one with him, the last one to see him in the park. And her husband, that wormy, rude, belittling man. He spoke to his wife with that snotty, accusatory tone. He was a cunt, there was no doubt about that, but that doesn't mean there wasn't something to what he said, or the way he said it.

Tommy began to speak to himself, inside his head, 'Get clear, Tommy boy… Don't let this worrying shit cloud your vision. Get it out of your head, get it out of your head and look for the clues, kid. Look for the clues.'

As he walked past Saint Monica's church on 79th Street, he saw a small group of mothers leaving the building. They said their goodbyes to one another, bundling up their small children from the bitter cold that had set in, as they left whatever children's event seemed to be happening that evening. "Love them ladies, love them with everything you have," he said, in a very low voice that no one could hear but himself.

Tommy arrived at his mother's building, walked up the steps of the stoop, and let himself in. He did what he could to shake his mind straight as he unlocked the door and entered his mother's apartment. She was sitting in front of the television, watching New York One news, and smoking a cigarette.

"Hey, Ma, how you doing today?" Tommy asked. She turned her head and looked up at him, a wide grin on her face at seeing him.

"Oh, Tommy. Tommy, how are you, Tommy? I'm fine, thanks. How was your day today, Tommy? Were there any good crimes for you today, Tommy?"

"Are there ever good crimes, Ma?"

"Oh, Tommy... You know what I mean, Tommy. Was there anything interesting today? I see a little boy went missing at John Jay Park today, Tommy. Do you know if they found him yet, Tommy?"

"No, Ma, I don't think so, and other than that today was a pretty boring day. Nothing cool, or interesting, to report at all today, Ma," he said, as he bent over her chair and kissed her on the head.

Tommy never was one to talk about his job to his mother, his wife, or his daughter. He felt strongly that the job, and the victims, were some kind of private matter between him and them, and besides worrying and upsetting the women in his life, he somehow found it disrespectful to the victims, and to himself. He would share stories with other cops, cops he knew understood. But overall, Tommy was pretty much a closed-mouth guy; he never really said anything if it didn't need saying. And right now his mother didn't need to know that Tommy had no clue where to look for this little boy. As he stood up from the kiss he had just given his mother he realized he was incredibly hungry and hadn't had anything since the oatmeal she made him more than 14 hours earlier.

"Did you eat anything tonight, Ma? I think I'm going to run over to Chef Ho's before they close for a little Chinese. Do you want to come along?"

"No, Tommy. No thank you, Tommy. I already had a little something to eat earlier, Tommy. Just maybe, maybe two hours ago, Tommy."

"Okay, Love. I'm just going to have a quick bite then, and I'll be right back home. I want to get a good night's sleep tonight, so I'll be back in a minute. Love you, Ma."

"I love you, Tommy."

Tommy turned and headed right back out the door. It was almost 10 PM and it was dark, and very cold. The temperature had dropped drastically during the day. He checked his phone and it was only eight degrees. 'Shit,' he thought, 'This is really cold for not even being Thanksgiving yet.' He buttoned up his coat and braced himself against the weather on his way up to Second Avenue.

As he turned the corner onto the avenue, he passed a small pub that was doing a brisk business of after-work Upper East Siders. The noise that tumbled out onto the sidewalk made it seem more like midnight on New Year's Eve, than ten in the evening on a Friday night. Tommy took note of a small, black and white dog tied to a sign post outside of the pub. The poor thing was wearing a brown sweater, but still shivered violently, either from the cold or possibly from the fear of being tied outside of a busy pub on a busy avenue.

"Fuckers… Who does that?" Tommy said out loud, as he passed the pub and the dog, as if to condemn the entire establishment for this small dog's fate.

***

Tommy took a seat near the window at a small, white-clothed table in Chef Ho's Chinese Restaurant. He ordered chicken with peanuts, pork fried rice, fried dumplings, and a Budweiser. He went over everything about the Hayden Marshall disappearance in his head. This time, in the calm, cool, methodical way he usually approached a case. He went over all the basics -- all the who's, what's, where's, and when's. He thought about the mother, the father, the other people in the park. He thought about everything, from every angle he could imagine. 'How could he just disappear?' he thought, 'He couldn't… The answers are there, they're always right there. Just think.'

He sat, ate, drank, and pondered for about forty-five minutes, not eating much of the food he had ordered. It all sat in front of him as his thoughts on the case kept distracting him from the meal. Then, with his meal barely touched, he asked for his check and left, still thinking about what he was missing as he started the walk back home.

As Tommy crossed 89th Street, he again saw the little dog, shaking in the cold. It was lifting one foot at a time, tap dancing, as if the pavement hurt its little feet. Tommy became very angry at the sight of this little dog, suffering the way it was, and he assumed it had been tied outside the pub for at least an hour now, on this below freezing night. He stopped and looked at the poor little thing, who stared straight past him to the door of the pub, waiting for its owner. There were two men and a woman near the entrance, smoking cigarettes, huddled up against the frigid weather themselves.

"Hey, this dog belong to any of yous?" He said, in a sharp and aggressive tone. All three looked rather surprised by the way he was talking to them, but all shook their heads no.

Tommy walked up to the door of the pub and pulled it open. The place was mobbed and was shoulder-to-shoulder with after work, Upper East Side professionals and Trust Fund hipsters. Tommy forced his way through the crowd and tried to get the bartender's attention, but the barman never looked up and Tommy couldn't catch his eye. Pissed off and frustrated, he exited the bar. He stood for a moment, as he looked at the small dog, and then started back to 88th Street. After turning the corner onto his block, he stopped.

"Motherfucker!" he said out loud. He turned and went back to the bar. As he approached the entrance, there were five or six new individuals outside smoking.

"This dog belong to any one of yous? ... Hey, you," he said to one woman who didn't respond to his initial question, "This your dog?" She shook her head no.

Tommy looked at the door of the bar and then back at the little dog, who was still tap dancing to keep his freezing paws off the cold concrete.

'Motherfucker!' Seemed to be the word of the night, as he stepped up to the dog, untied him, and picked him up. Tommy unbuttoned the top two buttons of his black leather coat, and stuffed the small dog, who couldn't have weighed more than 12 pounds, inside, hoping to warm it up.

"Motherfucker," he said again, out loud, as he continued home to his mother's apartment and then once again, "Mother…fucker!" as he approached the building, startling a couple as he passed them.

Tommy unlocked the door and entered the apartment. His mother looked over and saw him pull the small dog from his coat.

"Tommy, what is that? What is that, Tommy? Is that a dog? Tommy? Are you bringing a dog into my house, Tommy?"

Tommy's mother never allowed him, or his sister Kathleen, to have pets in the apartment when they were growing up. She never wanted to deal with any animals, their mess, or their expense. She wasn't an animal hater of any sort, she just never saw a good reason to have one, and therefore they never did.

"Yeah, Ma. Some asshole had it tied up outside in the cold. I couldn't leave the poor thing out there. I looked for the owner, but couldn't find him. Look at this poor little thing; he's frozen to the bone."

"Tommy, what are you gonna do with it, Tommy? I don't want a dog here, Tommy," the old girl said firmly.

"No, no, Ma, I'm not keeping this thing. I just couldn't leave it out there."

He held the dog in one hand, as it shook off the cold in the warm apartment.

"Is it a boy or a girl dog, Tommy?" His mother asked, as she got up from her recliner to take a closer look at the pup.

"I don't know, Ma," Tommy replied. He lifted it up and looked. "He's a little boy dog, Ma."

"What's his name, Tommy?"

"How the fuck do I know what his name is, Ma? I only picked him up two minutes ago."

"Tommy, don't you talk to me with that language, Tommy."

"Sorry, Ma... I'm sorry, I am. It's been a long day, Ma, and I'm upset about this little fella and whatever lowlife would leave him out in the cold like that. I'm sorry, Ma, you know I didn't mean anything by that."

"I know, Tommy, I know... Just remember who it is you're talking to, Tommy. Do you think he's hungry, Tommy?"

"I don't know, but I'm sure the little guy would love to eat something. I think dogs always like to eat."

"Okay, Tommy, I'll fix him up a little something, Tommy."

She went to the kitchen and scrambled up two eggs and fried two slices of bacon. She cut the bacon up and mixed it in with the eggs. The little black and white dog ate it all, in about eight seconds flat, and looked up at Tommy and his mother. Then he urinated on the kitchen floor.

"Ohhh, Tommy!" his mother said, with a lilt in her voice, "Do you think he's gonna do that every time?"

"I don't think so, Ma, and there won't be many more of these times anyway. I'll get him outta here and somewhere else tomorrow."

***

Tommy got ready for bed, and then fixed the little dog a bed on the floor, in his room. He put a pillow down and one of his old hooded sweatshirts, which had 82nd Airborne printed across the front. He placed a small bowl of water on the floor next to it and put the dog into the little makeshift bed he created. He stepped over to his own bed and when he turned to sit down, the dog was standing at his feet looking up at him. Tommy picked the little dog up, put him back in the sweatshirt bed, and returned to his own bed. Once again, when he turned to sit down, the little dog was at his feet.

"Listen, that's your bed, little guy. Go to bed... bed, okay? I'm not going to keep putting you in there. Stay in there and go to sleep. Just stay there, okay?"

Tommy then slid himself under the blankets and turned out the light.

Sixty seconds later, he felt the little dog scratch at the edge of the patchwork quilt that hung from the side of the bed.

Scratch scratch scratch... scratch scratch scratch.

Tommy touched the button on his cell phone, which gave a minimal amount of light to the pitch-black room, got out of bed, and put the dog back onto the sweatshirt bed. He returned to his own bed. About sixty seconds went by and again:

Scratch scratch scratch... scratch scratch scratch.

Tommy reached over the side of the bed, grabbed the little dog by the scruff of his neck, and lifted his tiny body into the bed. "Listen. This is a one-night deal, you got that? And if you shit or piss in this bed, I will shoot you, okay? So be a good little guy and go to sleep."

The little pup sat for a minute, then pushed himself up under the blankets and into Tommy's chest, curling himself into a tight ball and falling fast asleep in a matter of seconds. Tommy rolled slightly and gently, so as not to disturb his new friend, and got into a position where he could cup the little dog with one hand as he lay tightly against Tommy's chest.

Tommy also soon fell asleep, with the warmth of this little dog soothing the pain and frustration of the day that was now behind him.

Chapter Four

Tommy woke early, with the little dog pushed tightly against his body. He lay motionless in bed staring up at the complete darkness for several minutes. 'Fuck me... Where are you little Hayden?' he thought to himself, 'Where can you possibly be?'

Tommy lay there for at least another 20 minutes staring into the dark, going over everything he knew about Hayden Jon Marshall, thinking about every angle he could go at this investigation from, wishing and praying for some clue, some piece of evidence to point him in the right direction. Tommy finally got up and threw on some sweats and sneakers. He grabbed his coat and stuffed his Smith and Wesson Centennial into the pocket. He looked at the little dog, who was lying still in the bed, watching Tommy's every move.

"Morning, little guy. How you doing today?" He picked up the dog's leash from the floor, attached it to his collar, and then set the dog on the floor.

The dog winced a little and lifted one of his front paws up. He then lifted one of his back paws, as if he were, again, trying to stay off of the cold concrete.

"Your feet bothering you, little guy?" Tommy asked.

Tommy lifted the dog up, tucked him under his arm and took him outside. It was a bitterly cold morning as the two stepped out onto the stoop. Tommy scanned the block from right to left, then walked down the steps, and set the little dog onto the sidewalk, hoping he would do his business. The little dog did nothing but stare up at Tommy, lifting one paw then the next, attempting to favor his obviously injured paws.

After about three minutes, Tommy picked up the dog and took him back into the apartment. He sat the little dog on his bed and examined his paws. When he touched the dog's front, right paw, the little dog winced and pulled away from Tommy. The same thing happened when he touched the dog's left rear paw.

"You poor little guy. Do your feet hurt you?"

Tommy set the dog onto the floor and walked a few paces back from where he sat him.

"Come here, little guy." He said softly. The little dog came to him but with an odd walk, obviously favoring his injured paws.

"This is no good. Your feet are really hurting you, aren't they?" Tommy said to the little dog, "Let's run up the street. Maybe they can help you out with these feet, and maybe they can find you a new home."

Tommy checked the time. He decided he had enough time to take the little dog up to the ASPCA on 92nd Street and possibly still make it to work on time. He went to the bathroom to shower and the dog followed him in and laid on the bathmat. When Tommy came out of the shower, he found a small puddle and a small pile, waiting for him in the corner of the room.

"What is this?" he said in a half angry tone as he dried himself with a towel, "Well, at least you're in the right room. And you didn't do it in front of Ma. I won't tell her if you won't," Tommy said to the little dog as he cleaned up his mess.

"Good morning, Tommy," his mother greeted him, as he exited the bathroom with the little dog. "Here, Tommy, here are another couple of eggs and bacon for the dog." She set a small plate with the food on the floor. The little dog ate it all, in less than eight seconds.

"He sure can eat, can't he, Tommy?" his mother exclaimed.

"He sure can," Tommy replied, as he stepped into his room to get dressed.

When he was ready to go, he kissed his mother goodbye, and then picked up the dog, tucking him inside his coat and under his arm.

"Tommy, are you taking that dog to work with you, Tommy?" his mother asked.

"No, Ma, I'm going to spin by the ASPCA before I head in, and drop the little guy off with them."

"Tommy, no, no, Tommy. They'll kill him there at the ASPCA, don't take him there."

"They won't kill him, Ma. They'll fix his feet and find him a nice home. They don't kill dogs at shelters anymore, Ma."

"Oh, Tommy… I don't know about that. You better make sure before you leave him there, Tommy."

"Okay, Ma, I'll make sure. Say goodbye to him now."

"Ohh, Tommy, look at his sweet little face. Goodbye sweet little boy and good luck," his mother said, putting her nose up against the little dog's nose while scratching him behind the ear.

Tommy left the building, with the little dog tucked under his arm, and walked up to the ASPCA on 92nd Street. The shelter was located in a large, new, red brick building, which had relocated from the much smaller facility that sat for years just down the block on the opposite side of the street. As soon as he entered the lobby, the receptionist-intake person greeted him. Tommy identified himself as a police detective and told her how he found the little dog, tied to a signpost, in the freezing cold. He explained that he took the dog home and this morning the dog was still having trouble walking.

The woman said it looked as though the dog may have gotten frostbite on his toes. She took the animal into the back room after having Tommy fill out some forms.

Tommy thanked the woman and headed toward the door. He stopped short, did an about face, turning back to the woman, and asked, "You guys don't still kill these animals, do you?"

The woman replied, "Actually, we do still euthanize animals, who we find to be unadoptable, yes."

"Oh... I didn't think that was a thing anymore."

"Unfortunately, it is," the woman replied with a sad smile and a nod, "There is only so much space here and way too many animals for us to care for," she added.

Tommy thanked her again and headed out the door. He grabbed a cab that was waiting in front of the Marriott Courtyard hotel next door and headed straight to the precinct, putting the little dog out of his mind, and little Hayden back to the forefront of his thoughts. On the ride down the thought of Hayden still missing again made his heartbeat faster and a sense of urgency, almost panic -- which was unusual for Tommy -- began to take over. 'Easy kid,' he said to himself, 'Be cool, man. Don't let your emotions cloud your vision, you're no good to Hayden if you're not thinking clearly.'

***

Tommy arrived at the station house on time and was the only one in the squad room, until Doreen arrived, and found Tommy sitting at her desk. She immediately led off with what she had found during her computer searches the evening before.

"Hi, Tommy, my search for child sex offenders last night came up with 14 hits in the area. Out of those, I narrowed it down to four who live within the confines of the precinct and had offenses against juveniles. One is in his 80's, and lives on 94th Street, another has moved to Long Branch, New Jersey, the other two are both living here in the two-one. One, as it happens, lives directly across the street from John Jay Park."

Tommy was paying full attention to everything Doreen was saying, but when she mentioned the last individual, living directly across the street from where Hayden Jon Marshall had gone missing, his spine straightened up and his eyes opened wider.

"Directly across the street? So what, what do you got on this guy?" Tommy said, in an excited manner.

"He's forty-nine years old, his name is Derek Spree, and he took a collar for possession of child pornography in '06. He copped a plea to ten years' probation and a sex rehab therapy program."

"What say we go pay Mr. Spree a visit," Tommy said, standing up and grabbing his leather coat, "hopefully we can catch him before he leaves home for the day."

***

07:58 AM, 533 East 78th Street

Tommy and Doreen parked in front of the fire hydrant on Cherokee Place, and walked to 78th Street, to Mr. Spree's building. It was an older building, constructed of yellow bricks, with a light green paint on all the window and door trim. It was exactly the same as every other building on that block. They walked up the couple of steps to the front door.

"There it is. That's his bell. Should we ring it, or try to get in by the super, or some other way?" Doreen asked.

"No, let's not announce ourselves. Let's see if we can find the super or…" and before he could finish, a woman opened the door on her way out, and both detectives smiled and walked in as she left.

Tommy stopped on the first floor by the steps leading upstairs and said to Doreen, "Let's play this cool, Doreen. We have no warrant. We'll say we're canvassing, in regards to a robbery that took place last night in the park, and see if we can gain entry. Once we get inside, it'll be all about scoping out some clues to see if Hayden is in the apartment, or has been in the apartment. Let's just dazzle this guy with some bullshit, long enough for a cursory search of the place, without this fucker catching on to what we're doing, okay?"

"Yup, I got it," Doreen replied.

They walked up the stairs to the second floor, and to Derek Spree's door. Tommy put his ear to the door and listened -- he could faintly hear what sounded like a television, or possibly a radio.

He put his hand up, with one finger over his mouth, motioning to Doreen to be silent. He waited and waited. It was only for a couple of minutes, but to Doreen it felt much longer. Nothing changed. Tommy heard nothing from the apartment, other than that low hum of a television or radio. Once satisfied that he wasn't going to hear anything of interest, he spoke very quietly to Doreen.

"We're going to knock, and when he answers, we're going to tell him that we are canvassing the building, asking about a robbery in the park. His windows face that way and he may have seen something. We're not going to mention Hayden at all. We'll see if we can get inside to ask him a few simple questions, and feel him out. Keep your eyes and ears open to anything that seems out of place, anything at all... I know you know this, Doreen, but sometimes the smallest things are the most telling. Mostly, I want to meet this guy and feel him out."

Doreen nodded.

Tommy knocked.

They waited.

Tommy knocked again.

"Hello, who is it?" A man's voice spoke behind the closed door.

"Hello, Mr. Spree? We are detectives from the 21st precinct, sir, here is my shield." Tommy held his detective shield up to the peephole. "There was a robbery in the park across the street last night, sir, and we'd like to ask you about it."

"A robbery? You think I robbed someone?" The voice asked, still not opening the door.

"No, sir, not at all. We'd like to ask you about some of the neighbors, some of your neighbors, sir. We know your windows face the park, so you may have some information that could help us."

"I don't think so, Detective, I don't know anything about any robbery."

"Sir, can you please open the door for us, sir? I really hate yelling through it, and I don't want your neighbors hearing our conversation this way either."

The locks began to tumble, and the door opened, about three inches.

"I don't know anything," Derek Spree whispered through the cracked door.

"Please, Mr. Spree, may we come in and talk for a moment?" Tommy asked, very calmly and politely.

"I don't, I really don't think it's necessary," Spree replied.

"It's very necessary, sir. This is a serious investigation and we have several questions we'd like to ask you, sir."

Spree mumbled, "Um uh, well uh, okay. Okay come in."

He opened the door. Derek Spree was an unbelievably average looking man. He was dressed casually, in a pair of tan Dockers, black running sneakers, and a brown cardigan, over a navy polo shirt. He stood about five foot, nine inches tall, had short brown hair that was parted on the side and was visibly uncomfortable to be met by the police, at his door, so early in the morning.

Both detectives entered the apartment, which was a large, one room studio, with windows facing 78th Street and the park. It was nicely furnished and clean. There was an unmade double bed that sat in the far corner, near the window. Next to the bed was a dresser and nightstand, and next to that, was a desk with a computer and large monitor. A matching sofa and chair set and a small coffee table were positioned opposite the desk. To the left was a tiny kitchen that could only fit a small table for two, and a door that opened to the bathroom.

Once inside, Tommy walked right past Derek Spree, and went straight to the windows.

"So, these are the windows that look out over the park?" Tommy asked, with his back to Mr. Spree. His eyes, unbeknownst to Spree, were darting all over the room.

"Uh, yes," Spree answered.

"Interesting," Tommy replied, continually looking everywhere, but facing the windows. "I bet the noise from kids playing in the playground right across the street, can be a pain though, am I right?"

"Uh, um, actually no, the kids don't bother me. I like children."

As Spree turned his attention to Tommy, and stepped toward the windows himself, Doreen also scanned the room. She looked for anything unusual and stepped toward the desk that held Spree's computer. She removed her phone from her pocket and began shooting photos of items she saw on Spree's desk, holding her phone low at her waist and shielding her actions with her body.

"I guess you do like children," Doreen added. "Wow... these are beautiful girls. Are they yours, Mr. Spree?" Doreen motioned to his desk, where he had numerous framed photographs of several different girls on his desk. There were well over a dozen more photographs thumbtacked to a cork board above the desk, all of them seeming to be between ten and twelve years of age.

"Uh, uh no... No, I don't have any children of my own. Those are my, uh, my uh nieces," Spree said as he turned away from Tommy and looked toward Doreen.

"They are all so pretty. Detective Keane, look at Mr. Spree's beautiful nieces. Jeez, you have a lot of nieces, Mr. Spree. How many are there?"

"Well uh, they're not all my nieces, just a few, a few uh, four of them are my nieces. The others are photos from their birthday parties and other events, and many of those girls are uh, are uh my nieces' friends."

"Oh okay, so these are your nieces, and your nieces' friends. So many of them. Looks like they have a good life with all these friends and birthday parties, pool parties, beach parties. So many events going on," Doreen said.

"Uh, well, yes they do. They do have great lives, yes."

"Mr. Spree, were you home yesterday?" Tommy asked. Spree whipped his head back to Tommy.

"Uh yes and well no, I was in and out... both in and out yesterday. I had to go out in the morning to--"

Doreen interrupted again, "I can't get over how beautiful all these young girls are, Mr. Spree, it's almost like you have a catalog for a modeling agency here."

"Why, uh, thank you... Uh," Spree replied, turning back to Doreen.

"Where did you have to go yesterday morning, Mr. Spree?" Tommy asked.

"Oh, yes, I had to go to the office yesterday morning actually, and I, and I have to go work now, as well."

"God, they are gorgeous," Doreen exclaimed again, distracting Derek Spree once again, causing him to jerk back and forth in confusion, trying to carry on both conversations with Tommy and Doreen simultaneously.

"So you work weekends? And where do you work, Mr. Spree?" Tommy inquired.

"I'm a, I'm a computer programmer for a gaming company, on 57th Street."

"Oh really? What's the name of the company?"

"It's a, it's called Gekovision. We do a lot of games for the Asian market."

"Interesting, do you like it?"

"I do yes, yes, I do like my job."

"So, you were gone all day yesterday?"

"Uh, um no, I was in and out. I left for the office, I don't know, about 8:30, 9:00 in the morning and came home by about 1:00 in the afternoon."

"Short day," Tommy said.

"Uh well, no, much of my work, I do here at home. I go into the office just for meetings mostly. What time... what time was this robbery you're asking about?"

"May I use your bathroom, Mr. Spree?" Doreen asked, interrupting yet again.

"Um uh, well I, uh... yes, yes of course you may," Spree replied.

"Okay, so you were out of the apartment, and at work, from nine in the morning till about one in the afternoon then, yes, Mr. Spree?"

"Uh yes, uh yes, that is correct... And what--"

"What did you do the rest of the evening, sir, once you came home?" Tommy asked.

"I worked here for a few hours, ordered in some Chinese food, and watched Netflix until about eleven at night. Then I went to sleep. But I never heard anything, or saw anything unusual last night, or yesterday. When… when exactly did this robbery occur?"

Doreen exited the bathroom with the sound of the toilet flushing. "Thank you so much, Mr. Spree," she said, once again distracting Spree from the conversation.

"Yes, yes of course, I… I--"

"Okay, Mr. Spree, I think we are all done here. Do you have a business card perhaps, with your number and email, in case we need to follow up at all?" Tommy asked.

"Uh, well uh, yes I do." Spree stepped over to his desk, picked up a card, and handed it to Tommy. "Here you go, I still don't quite understand, what exactly--"

Tommy interrupted, "That's alright, Mr. Spree. We are so sorry to bother you this morning, sir. You've been more than helpful. If we need to follow up at all we will get in touch with you by phone or by email."

"Um uh, okay, but I don't, I don't understand what--"

As Tommy and Doreen walked out of the door, Doreen interrupted Spree one more time.

"Yes sir, thank you for your time and for the use of your bathroom, Mr. Spree. You've been a big help today, sir."

"Help? What did, what did you even ask me?" Spree's last words were muffled a bit, as the door to the apartment closed.

***

"Excellent, excellent job, Doreen. I like how you kept him off balance the whole time we were in there. That fucker is still scratching his head trying to figure out what happened," Tommy said, with a laugh, as they left the building.

"Thanks, Tommy, but are we any closer to finding Hayden? I didn't see anything in that apartment that made me think of Hayden, did you? That Spree is definitely a perv, with all those photos of little girls up on the walls, and on the desk, but I didn't see anything that said Hayden, did you?"

"No. I didn't see anything either or we wouldn't be leaving so soon, or without that creep in cuffs. I also didn't see anything that would give us cause for a search warrant, but we're gonna check this fucker Spree out today. We now know where he works, and his supposed alibi. Let's see if we can find his old probation officer. See if there's anything he can share... My feeling is this fucker is up to no good. Whether or not he's our man, or knows anything about Hayden Marshall, is another question. But I definitely don't like his vibe, I'll tell you that."

"God no, me either. Knowing his priors and seeing all those little girls on the walls really gave me a bad feeling, Tommy, it actually made me a little ill."

"Well, you didn't show it, kid. Good job, you really had him on the ropes the whole time."

Tommy and Doreen walked across the street and climbed into their car. Doreen closed the door, and shifted in her seat to face Tommy, continuing to talk.

"I don't like this creepy perv one bit, with his mild-mannered way and Mr. Rogers sweater. Here, look," she showed Tommy her phone, "I was able to get photos of all the girls he had posted on his wall and desk, when he followed you towards the window."

"Doreen, you sneaky thing you. Great job!"

"And look, these are more photos he had of young girls, framed in his bathroom. Nieces my ass! None of these girls are the same girl, from what I could tell. Look, none of them appear to be the same girl twice -- they're all just a collection of his favorite little girls... I hate to think of what goes through this creep's head. Or what he may be up to. Also here, here are a couple of other business cards I took from his desk. This is the one he gave you, and here are three others from other people. I took a couple more photos of some papers on his desk as well, and in the bathroom I got everything he had in his medicine cabinet and under his sink. And look, look here, that is a prescription bottle of Ketalar."

"Ketalar?"

"Yeah, Ketalar, you know Ketamine? Special-K."

"Fuck, that horse tranquilizer they use as a date rape drug? That dirty fucker."

"Yeah, that's the stuff."

"Excellent job, Doreen, you did great, absolutely great in there. We're gonna look hard into Spree and see what he's up to. I gotta say though, I don't feel any further along with this investigation. Let's head over to the Marshalls' place and see if they have anything else for us."

***

Tommy and Doreen arrived at the Marshall's building, on 79th Street, and made their way up to the apartment. After Tommy knocked, Jessica Marshall answered the door, looking about ten years older than she had the day prior.

"Hello, uh um, good, good morning, Detectives. How, uh, how are you today?" She stated in a dull monotone manner.

"Fine, Mrs. Marshall, thank you. We stopped by to see how you were making out and let you know we are on the case looking for Hayden," Tommy replied.

"Yes, yes thank you, please come in," she offered with her eyes half open.

"Are you alright, Mrs. Marshall?" Tommy asked.

"I am, well no, no I am not handling this very well at all... not at all." She began to cry as her legs gave way and her knees began to buckle. Both Tommy and Doreen caught her and kept her from falling to the floor, and the two detectives helped her to the same spot on the couch where they had sat the day before.

"Are you okay, Jessica?" Doreen asked, "Can I get you a glass of water or some tea maybe?"

"No, no thank you. I just need to sit," she replied.

Doreen, noticing large bruises on her left arm, asked, "What happened to your arm here, Jessica?"

"That? Oh that... I uh, I uh banged myself on the bathroom door yesterday, that's all." Jessica had her head lowered, with her hair dangling in her face.

"Are you sure, Jessica?" Doreen asked again, in a slightly firmer tone. "And where is Mr. Marshall today? Is he home?"

"No, no, he went to his sister's last night. We had a fight and he left to go stay at his sister's last night."

"Jessica... Mrs. Marshall, look at me. Did your husband put these marks on your arm?" Doreen asked outright this time.

"No, no I ran into the door, that's what, that's how I got bruised up there," she began to cry again, "We just had a big fight again... and then he left to his sister's. He doesn't hit me, we just fight, that's all."

"Do you fight a lot?" Doreen asked.

"Yeah... yes, yes we do. He yells at me and we fight a lot," she replied semi sobbing.

"Why Jessica? Why do you fight so often?"

"Because... because, well, he's just mean to me... and because, because I'm a bitch. I don't know why, really, we are just so dysfunctional, I know I'm a bitch... I know it, and he, he has no self-control and gets mad at everything, and takes it out on me, and then I antagonize him... I know I do... Our therapist isn't helping us. I don't know if she can." She continued to sob, putting her hands over her face.

"Are you on any medication today, Mrs. Marshall?" Tommy asked.

This question made Jessica stop her sobbing and look up at Tommy, her eyes glassy and swollen.

"Yes. Yes, I took some, some Xanax last night... and this morning. You see, because I couldn't sleep, and I can't, haven't slept, and my husband is at his sister's, my Hayden is still missing and I don't know where he is. Oh god, oh god my Hayden." She covered her face with her hands and again began to sob, Doreen took her in her arms on the couch, as they sat the day before, in an attempt to comfort her.

Tommy went to the kitchen and got her a glass of water. A few minutes went by and Jessica Marshall wiped her eyes, the cry seeming to sober her up a little.

"Mrs. Marshall, Detective Doyle and I have some work to go and do to locate Hayden for you. We wanted to stop by and make sure you were okay and if you had possibly heard anything or had any new information for us. So we're going to head out now, but we will be in touch again, very soon, okay?"

"Yes, yes please, please go find my son."

***

As Tommy and Doreen made their way out of the apartment and to the elevator, Doreen stated, "Bathroom door my ass."

"Yeah, it got a little rough in there last night, I imagine. Like I said earlier, these things tear families apart."

"Little fucker," Doreen mumbled. "What now, Tommy?"

"Italian Village is around the corner. Let's grab a slice and then head back to the precinct and see what we can dig up on Mr. Spree."

"Sounds good."

The two drove up to First Avenue and made the right, pulling into the bus stop to park and headed into the Italian Village Pizzeria.

Tony, the boss, came around from behind the counter to say hello and give a handshake to the detectives, but upon seeing both were in somber moods, he kept his greeting short and spared them any small talk.

Doreen ordered a slice with mushrooms, and a diet Snapple iced tea, and Tommy asked for two slices with sausage, fresh garlic, black olives, and a can of Pepsi. They took a seat at a table up front near the window and they both ate quickly. Their only conversation was about Derek Spree.

"Do you think it could be him, Tommy?" Doreen asked, wiping sauce from the corner of her mouth.

"It could most definitely be him, but the problem at the moment is, one… we have zero evidence pointing us to him, and two… it looks like he likes little girls and not little boys. But right now, until something breaks, we have nothing else. So at the very least we have to dig into him enough to decide either to go after him or cross him off the list."

"Right, right," Doreen replied, somewhat disheartened, as she finished her slice and took a sip of her tea.

Chapter Five

Back in the squad room, both detectives began searching for anything they could find on Derek Spree. Doreen, who had considerably better computer skills than Tommy, ran his name every which way she could, and searched through every social media platform she could think of.

Tommy contacted Derek Spree's probation officer, who stated he was a model probate, with zero violations and a good long-term job history. Tommy also ran him through the NYPD database, ran his name, date of birth, and located every known address, every vehicle he ever owned, his high school, college, several employers, and together, they found nothing. Other than the one prior arrest and conviction for possession of child pornography in 2006, they found not even a single parking ticket.

After several hours filled with computer searches, phone calls, and cross-checking, both Tommy and Doreen felt like they had even less than when they started their day.

"Fuck me!" Tommy exclaimed loudly, every head in the squad room turning to face him, and Sergeant Browne poking his head out from his office. Tommy was usually so quiet, and closed-mouth; an outburst like this startled the entire squad room. Leaning back in the chair and running his hands through his hair, he said "I'm here banging away on this fucking computer all afternoon and nothing. This kid is out there in the world, suffering who knows what, and I got nothing... and now here we are and it's end of tour and we got nothing, Doreen. All day shot and not a fucking thing, nothing!"

Sergeant Browne closed the door to his office, and Detectives Stein and Colletti continued with their own caseloads once Tommy's outburst was over and they realized there was nothing they could do.

"I know, Tommy, I know," Doreen replied softly with a heavy and desperate tone, "And I'm fried, Tommy, I can't think of another thing we can search. I think we, I'm afraid we have hit a wall and need to return to this tomorrow."

"I'm afraid I have to agree with you, Doreen. I have nothing else I can think of to look at right now. I'm fucking lost here."

"Go home, Tommy. Grab some dinner and get some sleep. Tomorrow we'll be better prepared to start again."

With that they both got up, signed out, said goodnight to Stein who was still sitting at his desk, and headed out the door. Saying goodnight one more time, they left the building and headed in opposite directions.

Tommy walked about ten blocks or so when he stopped and hailed a cab.

"85th and York, near left corner, please," he told the driver as he climbed in. He wasn't up for the walk, and thought a Jameson and a Budweiser at Bailey's Corner Pub may help him relax and clear his head.

About three minutes into the ride Tommy spoke up again. "No, no driver, take me to 92nd and First, near right corner, please."

After leaving the cab on the corner, Tommy walked the 30 yards to the ASPCA, where he had been that morning. He entered the building and waited to speak to the receptionist, a different woman than the one who was working earlier. He identified himself and asked about the little dog that he brought in that morning. The receptionist told him she had no information but would get someone to help him.

She returned, with a young woman wearing scrubs who had her hair pulled back in a tight ponytail. Tommy again identified himself as the man who dropped off a little black and white dog sometime around six in the morning. He told the woman the story of how he had found the dog, tied up outside to a signpost, tap dancing on the concrete and how he was unable to find its owner.

The woman commended him, "Well, Detective, by bringing him here you most likely saved this dog's life," she continued, "Although he had a sweater on, Boston Terriers have very little hair, and they aren't built for extreme weather -- neither the extreme cold nor the extreme heat -- and the reason he was tap dancing, as you put it, is because his feet were literally freezing on the pavement. Unfortunately, we had to amputate two of his toes, one from one of his front paws, and one from one of his rear paws."

"Oh no!" Tommy exclaimed, "Will he be alright?"

"Yes, yes he is going to be just fine. He's already recovered from the surgery, and is in really good spirits."

"Well, I think I'd like to take him with me if I can. What do I need to do to do that?" Tommy asked.

"Really? Well that would be wonderful, Detective Keane! Here, let me get you a little paperwork, and while you fill this out, I'll go and get him ready to go."

And that was it. In less than a half an hour Tommy was stepping out of the ASPCA on 92nd Street, with a small Boston Terrier puppy stuffed inside his leather coat.

And somehow... somehow, this was a small victory for the day. He still felt at a complete loss over Hayden Marshall, and both he and Derek Spree were in the forefront of his thoughts, but somehow removing this injured little puppy from a cage in the ASPCA was a minor win on this long and seemingly wasted day for Tommy.

'But what about Spree?' he again began to think about the day's events on his walk home to his mother's. 'What is up with this fucker? He's dirty, he's definitely up to no good, but is he tied to Hayden at all? Doreen and I ran him every which way, we've gone through all of his social media, and nothing, we haven't turned up anything. How can I find more? How can I get a warrant for his apartment and his phone and computer if I have no evidence to present a judge? How?'

His walk went quickly, as he again went over everything he knew about the case, and that knowing feeling, that feeling that there was something nearby, almost at his fingertips crept in. He didn't like Mrs. Marshall for this, but was he wrong? He did very much think Derek Spree was up to his neck in something nefarious, but could he be attached to Hayden at all? He really wasn't liking him for this disappearance either.

'I need a warrant to get into Spree's computer. I got nothing, no probable cause on this guy, a few photos on the wall and a prior will get me nothing in front of a judge. Fuck a warrant, if this filthy kiddie porn fuck is up to something -- anything, Hayden Marshall related or not -- I need to find out.'

He continued to speak to himself inside his head, almost in an encouraging tone, trying to talk himself into some sort of new approach.

Tommy arrived at his mother's place on 88th Street, unlocked the door and walked into the apartment.

"Ma...Ma... You were right," is how he decided to begin his explanation as he walked into the apartment, "They do still euthanize animals at the ASPCA." He pulled the puppy out of his leather coat and continued, "So, I decided to--"

"Ohh, Tommy, you brought the little boy back, Tommy! Ahhh, look at that sweet little face, Tommy. I told you, Tommy, I told you!" Maria exclaimed happily from her recliner as Tommy handed the puppy to her.

"Listen, I know you don't want him here, but I promise, I will find him a good home in the next couple days, Ma. I just couldn't leave him there, I just couldn't, Ma."

"Of course you couldn't, Tommy. I raised a good-hearted man, Tommy. You couldn't leave this beautiful little boy there to be killed, Tommy. No, you did the right thing like you always do, Tommy. Tommy? Tommy? What are these bandages on his feet for, Tommy?"

"He had to have a couple of toes removed, Ma. They were frozen, frostbitten, so the vets at the ASPCA had to remove them."

"Oh no, Tommy, this poor little boy! You poor little boy," she repeated, putting her nose up against the little dog's, "Well, of course you can stay here until we find you a home, you beautiful little boy."

As Tommy watched his mother coo over the twelve-pound black and white little dog in her lap, Tommy was struck with an idea. A flash, like in a cartoon where a light bulb goes off over one's head.

"Ma! I'll be right back, I'll be right back. I have to do something," Tommy said as he was already making his way down the hallway.

"Okay, Tommy," Maria Keane replied, not taking her eyes from the puppy in her hands.

Tommy left the apartment and took the steps, two at a time, from his mother's apartment on the second floor, up to the fourth floor. When he reached the Sarhadi's apartment, he stopped, took a deep breath, cleared his head for a second and then knocked, waited a second or two, then knocked again.

"Who is there?" A stern voice came from behind the door. Tommy immediately recognized it as that of Bita Sarhadi, Roya's mother.

"Hello, Mrs. Sarhadi, it's me, Tommy Keane from downstairs."

The three locks on the door began to click and clack as they tumbled into their unlocked position.

Bita opened the door almost fully, looking very business-like in a black turtleneck, grey tailored slacks, black high heeled shoes, and a pair of expensive looking glasses on a silver chain hanging around her neck. Her dark hair was pulled up in a high bun. She held a strong and regal stance, half inviting and half threatening, as she stood in front of Tommy.

"Hello, Tommy. What do you want?"

"Hey, Mrs. Sarhadi, how you doing? I'm hoping to speak with Roya, if she's home."

"You may call me Bita, we are both adults and I know you for many years. Roya is not home," Bita replied in her forceful monotone way.

"May I ask you to give her my card, and have her call me as soon as she can, please?"

"Of course," was her simple reply.

"Thank you very much, Bita," Tommy handed her his card, "And how have you been, Bita? It has been a long time since I saw you last."

"I will give her the card," Bita replied, and then they both stood there, face to face in the doorway for a moment. Oddly, Tommy, the hardened detective who usually made people uncomfortable for a living, was the one feeling awkward in this moment as Bita stared at him expressionless after her scant reply.

"Uh, okay great. Thank you, Bita, I appreciate it," Tommy said and then stepped back from the door.

"Goodnight, Tommy. Give your mother my regards," Bita said as she slowly closed the door, still standing almost motionless, a handsome statue of a beautiful, but bitter woman.

"I will, thank you."

Tommy made his way down the stairs to his mother's apartment, opened the door and stepped inside. His mother was sitting in her recliner, watching television with a cloud of cigarette smoke hanging above her head. She greeted Tommy immediately, but never took her eyes off the television set. As she spoke, the little black and white dog leapt from her lap, and let out a little yelp as he hit the hardwood floors, his paws sore from his surgery. He ran as fast as he could to meet Tommy at the door.

"That was quick, Tommy. And I didn't ask you earlier, Tommy, how was your day today, Tommy? I didn't ask you about your day," his mother repeated.

But Tommy first replied to the little black and white dog. "Hello little guy, are you happy to see me?" he asked, as the dog attempted to climb up Tommy's leg. Bending over and picking him up, he answered his mother, "It was okay, Ma, nothing interesting to share. How was your day today?"

"JoJo, Tommy."

"What's that, Ma?"

"JoJo, Tommy, JoJo. That's the dog's name now, Tommy. We're calling him JoJo, Tommy."

"No, Ma, you can't name him, it's only been ten minutes. And besides, if you name him it's going to be harder for you when we get rid of him. And JoJo, what kind of name is that for a dog? No." Tommy smiled, and then began to laugh a little, as he spoke.

"No, Ma, you didn't, you didn't. You named him after Joey Farrell? Ha ha ha… that's too rich, Ma. You named him after Joey "No Toes" Farrell? That is too funny, ha, thanks, Ma, that makes me laugh," holding the little dog closer to his face, he looked at him, "Ha, little JoJo, you like your new name little guy? Well it certainly fits, I guess. And old JoJo No Toes, wasn't a bad guy, was he, Ma?"

"No, Tommy, JoJo was a good man, and I felt it seemed appropriate, Tommy," his mother stated, letting out some smoke from her last cigarette drag as she said it.

***

Joseph "Joey" or "JoJo No Toes" Farrell, lived a few buildings up the block from the Keane's building on 88th Street. He was a biker, a broad-shouldered, heavily tattooed, big- bearded biker, who belonged to a one percenter outlaw biker gang called "The Devil's Avengers." His entire chest, back, and shoulders were covered in tattoos, stopping at his upper arms, where a typical T-shirt sleeve would end, and at his neck along the lines of where a V neck shirt would end. There were dozens of tattoos, possibly hundreds, and they were all done in that old fashioned, indigo blue tattoo ink, that you never see used anymore. Pieces of old school flash covered his torso; so many that, if you saw him shirtless in the summer, which was often the case on East 88th Street, from a distance you would think he was wearing a blue V neck t-shirt.

The only tattoos he had outside of this V neck sea of ink, was a faded heart that said "mother" on his left forearm, and an eagle holding an anchor on his right forearm with U.S.N. above it, and NEVER AGAIN below it.

Despite Joey Farrell's dangerous and menacing appearance, he was a very affable man, who always presented himself as a gentleman regardless of his looks, and took care to keep an eye out for everyone on the block, as if they were all extended family.

Joey, who worked as an Ironworker for local 580, as much of the neighborhood did, lost four of his toes when a giant, several-thousand-pound container loaded with windows came loose from the straps that were holding it while a crane maneuvered it, and crushed them right off of his foot.

From that day forward, Joey Farrell became known as JoJo No Toes. Joey Farrell passed at the age of 62 from a heart attack in 2007. He was a much-loved character in the neighborhood and had been missed since his passing. And now a little black and white dog who lost a couple toes to frostbite, due to a selfish and uncaring asshole of an owner, would carry his name as a tribute.

***

As Tommy continued speaking with his mother, his cell phone went off. Not recognizing the number, he answered it simply, "Keane."

"Hi, Tommy, it's Roya. My mother told me you wanted to speak to me?"

"Oh hey, Roya, how you doing? Yes, I would like to speak to you. I want to ask you something, but it's a bit complicated to get into over the phone. Do you think we can maybe meet up tomorrow, maybe for a minute, before you go to work, or later when you come home? Grab a cup of coffee or something? I should only need a few minutes of your time."

"Yeah, my mother called me, saying you came to the door and I needed to call you right away. Yeah sure, I'll be available. I'm on my way home right now and will be available all night if you like? I usually don't go to bed until about 11:30, 12:00, if you're not busy tonight?"

"Really? Yeah, that would be great, Roya."

"Okay cool, I'll be home in less than ten minutes."

"Great, have you eaten yet? Would you like to go around the corner to Chef Ho's for a bite and we can discuss what I want to discuss with you?"

"Hells yeah! That would be perfect, I haven't eaten yet and I am starving. Do you want to meet there in like ten minutes? Will that work?"

"Definitely. I'll see you there in ten. Looking forward to it." Tommy hung up and handed little JoJo back to his mother, where he sat up straight and attentive, in her lap.

"Where you off to now, Tommy? Eating at Chef Ho's again, Tommy?"

"Yes, Ma'am. Would you like me to bring something back for you, Ma?"

"No thanks, Tommy. I already ate, Tommy, but thank you, Tommy."

"Okay, Ma. I'll be back in a bit, love you," Tommy kissed his mother on the head, and gave little JoJo a scratch under the chin, "You be a good boy for Ma now, JoJo. Ha... JoJo, that's funny Ma, that's really funny."

"He's always a good boy, Tommy," His mother replied, almost in defense of the little dog.

Hayden Jon Marshall

Chapter Six

Tommy arrived at Chef Ho's restaurant, and was greeted by the familiar face of one of the older waiters, who sat Tommy in his preferred seat, in the corner by the front window.

"Two time this week, good," the waiter said, giving Tommy a thumbs up and a big smile.

"Well, you guys do it right here," Tommy replied, smiling at the old man.

No sooner had Tommy sat down, than Roya walked in. She bypassed the hostess stand and went straight to the table where she saw Tommy sitting. He stood and she approached and gave him a kiss on the cheek, removed her black canvas shoulder bag from around her torso, along with her jacket, hanging them both on the back of her chair as she sat down across from Tommy.

"So... this is intriguing, Tommy. What do you want to ask me, that you would call a meeting with me like this -- what do you neighborhood guys call it? A sit down?" Roya grinned as she leaned forward towards Tommy and rested her forearms on the table.

"Ha, yes, a sit down. Well, it's a little complicated, Roya, I have to ask you for some computer advice. I know you have always been a bit of a computer nerd... sorry... wiz? And I need to be guided in the right direction, as my computer skills are really shit, but like I said it's a little complicated. So, what say we order, and then I'll explain, cause it may take a little while."

"Okay cool. What you wanna do? Are we gonna order individually, or are we gonna do the share share thing?"

Tommy smiled. He hadn't seen Roya for several years, and although she was now a grown woman, he could still see the teenager who used to babysit his daughter on occasion, and the little girl he had watched grow up in the same building for her entire life. And now, here she was, a beautiful, intelligent young woman, from whom he needed advice. Still, she spoke to him like the fifteen-year-old he knew ten years before.

"Share share of course. You pick an entrée for us, and I'll pick an entrée for us, and we can share some dumplings and fried rice?"

"Bet! That's how I like to do it, too," she replied.

When the older waiter returned, with a pot of hot green tea and their waters, Roya ordered the chicken with broccoli. Tommy ordered the Kung Pow chicken, along with the fried pork dumplings and the pork fried rice.

"Listen, it's been forever since I've seen you, and I want to know everything about you and your life, but right now, I really need to ask you about some computer stuff. I'm hoping you can maybe tell me something that can help me out a little?"

"Okay, shoot," Roya replied, taking a sip of the hot tea.

"Alright, well…" Tommy paused, "Like I said, it's a little complicated and I thought of you, well really, I thought of you because I just saw you yesterday, I guess. But I remember how sharp you were when it came to technology, and computers, and I have this investigation going on. There's this missing little boy, and…" Tommy paused again, "Well, I'm not allowed to do what I want to do, so what I am going to ask you about, well it's illegal, and I don't want you to do anything, but I am hoping you can help point me in the right direction, in how to do this thing I wanna do, if I can. Maybe you can tell me what equipment I may need, if there is any, and again point me in the right direction as far as some gear and techniques."

Roya looked at him for a second, "Listen, Tommy, I know it's been years, but I have always looked up to you, almost like an older brother maybe. I trust you, more than any man I have ever known, and I trust that whatever it is you are talking about must be important or you wouldn't be talking to me, but what exactly are you looking to do? You're going to have to tell me what it is exactly so I can know if I can help you or not."

"Okay, obviously this conversation can't leave this table."

"Of course, no need even to ask, that goes without saying."

Tommy sat for a moment in silence, staring at Roya. He took a deep breath and let it out as he leaned his elbows on the table, leaning in towards Roya.

"I have this missing little boy I'm looking for, and we can't find anything on him, but we have a computer programmer pedophile, with a child porn conviction, who lives across the street from where this little boy went missing. We have nothing PC wise -- Probable Cause wise -- we can go after him for, other than photos of children all over the walls of his apartment. We've gotten into everything we can, computer wise, without a warrant, which is really nothing but his social media stuff and public records, which are all clean. With nothing to go on for probable cause, I'm shut down on this guy. So what I want to do is figure out how I can hack into his computer... Is this something you can explain to me? Is there any product I can buy to help me hack into someone's computer? I assume there are some skills needed, but what are they? Is this something you can help me out with? This fucker is dirty, I am sure of that."

Roya looked at him, rather sternly, as she thought for a moment. She stared at him in a way that resembled her mother, in a regal, almost condescending, manner... then a small smile.

"Listen, Tommy," her smile grew a bit, almost as though she were laughing at him, "I could definitely, possibly, upgrade whatever computer you have, to be able to search things out more thoroughly, and protect you from other eyes looking at you, and seeking you out for what it is you want to do here. I could also teach you how to do in-depth searches and how hacking works. I do have knowledge in these areas. However, neither of us have the time for that. If this guy is a computer tech and any good at his job, and has any decent computer skills, all his illegal kiddy porn or any criminal behavior he does, will be conducted on the dark web..."

"And what is the dark web exactly? I have an idea but-"

"Exactly. This is what I'm getting at; you're just too old and out of touch for this, Tommy. If I told you exactly what to do, and how to do it, you would never have the skills to pull it off. Certainly not in time to save any little boy, plus you'd probably end up getting yourself in trouble, and fired, or put in jail, all at the same time."

"Well, I don't have a choice, kid," Tommy said, with a slight lilt of desperation, "I have to get into this guy's computer somehow."

"Well, listen. I can still help you out, Tommy."

"No, no, I can't have you getting yourself involved in this."

"Really?" Her stern mother's look came over her face again, and her voice became a little more monotone, "Really, Tommy, didn't you involve me the second I walked in here and sat down? Did you not make me what you cops call... an accessory-to? Listen, Tommy, I'm a big girl now. I know about this stuff, it's my job to defend against it, and I'm paid pretty well to keep it from happening to a multi-billion dollar company. I also know people who are involved in all sorts of dark web activities...You want some help? You want someone you can trust? You want someone who is on your side, Tommy? Well, here I am big brother. Tell me what you need."

Tommy sat back in his chair. He looked into Roya's deep brown eyes. She was, in a flash, no longer a fifteen year-old, or a twenty-five year-old indie rocker heading out for a video shoot. She looked back at him with those big brown eyes, and she was deadly serious, and he knew it. The confidence of her stare somehow strengthened Tommy's resolve and in that second a partnership was formed.

(Tommy gave her one last chance to walk away.)

"Listen, Roya, this is serious business and--"

"Enough. You need me, this little boy needs me, and possibly other children need me. So that's it, I'm in, one hundred and ten percent, I'm in. Now it's up to you to give me what I need on this guy you want to hack."

"What do you need?" Tommy asked.

"Everything you have. Absolutely everything you have and anything new you can find. I'm going to guess this is like one of your detective investigations, and you have no idea exactly what will help me get to where I need to go, sort of like Son of Sam. Every cop in the city was searching for him, and how did they catch him? They caught him with a parking ticket... So give me everything. You'd be surprised what is out there on the web, and what connects with what."

Tommy smiled, but it was a sad smile. He loved Roya, he had known her for her entire life, he had watched her grow, she babysat his daughter, and now he had just dragged her into a crime, and asked her to commit one herself.

"Okay, you'll get everything, anything you need, including any money you may need."

"I don't want money for this, Tommy," she said, with a bit of anger in her tone.

"For any equipment or gear you may need."

Roya smiled that laughing smile again, "Oh okay. No I won't need anything, Tommy. Just his info, all of it, and, some time."

"How long will it take to get into his system, do you think?"

Roya shrugged, "Could take hours, could take days? I have no idea where I'm going with this until I get started."

"I understand… and Roya," he reached across and grasped her hands that sat folded on the table, "Thank you."

The waiter brought the dumplings and placed them on the table, and the seriousness of the conversation was broken. Tommy picked up a dumpling with the stainless-steel tongs and placed one on Roya's plate.

"Thank you, Tommy," Roya said.

"You are very welcome, Roya. Would you like a puppy?"

"What? Where did that come from? And no, my mother would never allow a puppy in the house."

Tommy then began the story of the last time he sat in this seat, just the day before, and how he ended up with a little black and white dog named JoJo. They both laughed, and reminisced, about JoJo No Toes Farrell, and so many other characters from the block and the neighborhood. They sat in Chef Ho's until they closed, then walked together back home.

***

After dropping Roya off at their building, Tommy walked back up to 2nd Avenue, where he caught a cab and headed down to the precinct. There he retrieved every piece of information he and Doreen had uncovered on Derek Spree, making copies of everything, and stuffing them in a folder. Then he headed back uptown. While in the cab, he texted Roya and told her he would text her again in about ten minutes, when he arrived to hand off the Spree dossier.

All went as planned, and Tommy thanked Roya again as they stood together, in the hallway where both of them had grown up, albeit twenty years apart. At that moment they entered into a pact to investigate a possible pedophile and kidnapper -- a scheme that could land them both in prison, but one that they thought was worth the risk.

Tommy, once again, started to explain the risk they were taking, and Roya smiled and told him, "Stop. We have a little boy to save, and possibly others as well. I'm not afraid, and I am more than capable."

Tommy stood silently for a moment and then he wrapped his arms around her in a hug so tight, Roya almost lost her breath. He released her from the hug, grasped both her shoulders with each of his hands, and kissed her on her forehead.

"You're a good woman, Roya. Be careful, kid."

He turned and walked back to his apartment, as Roya replied, "I will, Tommy. Trust me, I will."

***

When Roya had stated she was "more than capable," it was in fact an understatement. Tommy, during dinner, had called her a "computer wiz" when, in fact, what Roya was, was a computer prodigy.

Roya, like both her parents, was born an exceptionally intelligent person. Growing up as the only child of a single mother, who was herself an accomplished chemist, Roya developed a very strong sense of self-discipline. Bita was Roya's only family, and role model, growing up. In school, Roya excelled in every class. In junior high, she was able to test into The Bronx High School of Science, an elite public high school, where she graduated fifth in her class.

Growing up in the burgeoning computer age, and being both encouraged and doted on educationally by her mother Bita, little Roya was a sponge when it came to computers. She learned everything there was to learn about them so quickly, that in high school she was years ahead of her instructors. While attending Hunter College on an academic scholarship, Roya, again, was ahead of her professors when it came to the curriculum -- so much so, that she felt college was a waste of her time. She viewed it simply as a formality just to receive a diploma, which of course was a necessity for her mother's sanity.

Roya was hired, immediately after graduating Hunter, by the IT department of a large finance company, with office buildings on Wall Street and in Midtown. Within six months, she was promoted out of IT to the role of Security Director, working under the CISO (Chief Information Security Officer). She was what is known as an ethical hacker, a computer security expert who specialized in testing the firm's own information systems.

By her second year of working for this company, she was considered one of the best on the team, and at 23 years old was earning just over $120,000 a year. But being young, and being interested in the world as a whole, Roya would also enter into ethically questionable hacking -- sometimes just for fun, other times she would join forums that would be considered more activist, or hacktivist, in nature.

Roya was also very proficient, and considered, in her underground world, to be a rather unique talent when it came to hacking.

Tommy had no idea who he had decided to approach. Here he had a chance meeting with a young woman he had known for all of her 25 years on earth. He knew she was bright, and very computer literate, and all he was asking for was a little advice. Did she know anything about hacking? Could she maybe point him in the right direction, and help him with some equipment?

So yes, she did laugh at his request during dinner. Tommy wasn't even on Facebook, and he could barely use the NYPD's system at work. He had zero chance of ever becoming anywhere near proficient at hacking, but his desperation to find Hayden Marshall was growing, and luckily for him, the one person he thought he could trust to ask for computer advice, was a pro and a prodigy.

Chapter Seven

Tommy's eyes snapped open to the total darkness of his room, with little JoJo in a ball, tightly pushed up against Tommy's side. He reached over to the nightstand for his phone: 45 minutes until the alarm rang. He turned off the alarm, and rolled out of bed and onto the floor, for his 50 morning pushups.

Two flights above him, Roya sat in her room, in front of two computers and a laptop. She had called in sick to work right after meeting Tommy in the hallway. She said she may have the flu and was running a fever, and might be more than a day or two.

She hadn't been to sleep yet. While Tommy and JoJo slept two stories below her, she typed away, looking for a path into Derek Spree's inner world. She had only been at it for about seven hours now, and she knew it could take many more hours, days, weeks, or even months. Derek Spree also had a computer background, and he certainly had reasons to be careful, and to cover his tracks.

What was now taking hold of Roya though, was anxiousness; this hack was different. There was a missing little boy involved, one who could be going through an unimaginable hell, one whose life may probably depend on Roya's ability to hack into this man's system.

This wasn't a mundane test of a financial system's ability to protect itself, or an abstract activist hashtag to save a species of bird she had never seen in Madagascar. This hack, this fight, was now becoming very real to Roya, more tangible than anything she had ever done in her life. She took this on in a split second, because of a long time loyalty to a neighbor who treated her kindly when she was a child -- someone who, yes she looked up to and admired, and maybe had a childhood crush on. But now the gravity of the situation, the seriousness of the case, had taken hold of her.

But Roya, true to her family roots, and maybe true to her neighborhood values, never once wavered in her decision. 'Fuck you Derek Spree,' she thought to herself, as she grew tired from lack of sleep. 'Fuck you, you dirty, filthy fuck. I will find out what you are up to. I will break your code, I will catch you, and Tommy will put you away forever, you creep, you fucking pedophile creep.'

Meanwhile, back on the second floor, Tommy came back in from walking little JoJo to find his mother up and making a cup of coffee for herself. The television was on across the room, with New York One News talking about a hit and run the prior night in Queens. As Tommy closed the door, his mother lit up a cigarette.

"Christ, Ma, it's a little early for one of those, isn't it? Why don't you knock it off with the smoking already? You're too smart to still be doing that, Ma."

"I'm never quitting, Tommy. You know I like it too much to quit, Tommy. Can I fix you some breakfast, Tommy?

Some oatmeal again, Tommy? Pancakes or French toast maybe, Tommy?"

"No thanks, Ma. I'm going to head into work a little early, I have a lot to do today."

He stepped across the kitchen and gave his mother a little hug and a kiss on the cheek.

"I love you, Ma, and stop that smoking will ya?"

"I'll think about it, Tommy."

'I'll think about it?' Tommy smiled to himself, knowing she was just humoring him. Maria Keane would sooner cut off her right arm than give up smoking and he knew it.

***

Tommy arrived at the precinct about 50 minutes before his shift began and the squad room was empty. He pulled out all the information he had collected on the Hayden Jon Marshall case. On a yellow pad he began writing down things he knew about the case, then things he didn't know but needed to know. There wasn't a lot of rhyme or reason to what he was doing, but it was an exercise he had learned from Detective Isaacs while working in the 5-3 squad. Isaacs would just write down things about the case, facts he knew, things he wanted to know, random things that seemingly made no sense but were attached to the case, and then read over them, and then he would redo the whole exercise. Isaacs would sometimes do this a dozen times, hell sometimes dozens of times, just to see what would pop into his head. It was like an abstract word puzzle. And every once in a while, he would strike gold. Tommy picked up the habit several years ago himself. He found it more of a way to meditate on the case, than an actual tool to solving crimes. But every detective has his own techniques, and he found that this one of Isaacs did help him on occasion.

As he scribbled and doodled thoughts onto his yellow pad, Sergeant Browne walked into the office.

"Good morning, Tom. Tell me you've cracked the Gillstone case, please."

"No, Boss, not yet. I've been putting all my efforts in on this missing kid," he replied, not looking up, still scratching stuff out on his pad.

"Listen, Tom," Sergeant Browne began softly with an understanding and concerned tone, "I know this is a missing three-year-old, and that the press has also reported on it, but hasn't it been over three days already? Why haven't you sent that one down to Missing Persons?" Browne questioned.

"No, Boss, today is the third day, so it's not three days yet."

Sergeant Browne stopped in the middle of the squad room and stared at Tommy, putting his hands on his hips and raising his voice slightly in an attempt to be more assertive.

"Well get rid of it, will you? You've got a ton of open cases you need to close, and the most pressing is that Gillstone case. That woman is relentless about us making an arrest."

"Well, she's just gonna have to fucking wait, isn't she?" Tommy replied in a deadpan tone of voice.

"What?" Sergeant Browne replied, in a somewhat surprised manner.

"You heard what I said. Mrs. Gillstone's earrings mean nothing to me. I have a missing three-year-old I need to find, I could give a fuck about her rich ass and her stupid earrings," Tommy said flatly.

"Hey, you listen. All of these cases are important, and the Gillstone's case is not only important but it holds weight. Do you know who Mr. Gillstone is? He's incredibly wealthy and very well connected, politically. Make an arrest on that case. And get rid of that missing, send it over to Missing Persons. That's why we have a Missing Persons Department, get it off your desk and out of this office."

Tommy replied only with a dead stare. He wanted to snap at Browne, but he knew it would be fruitless, and really unnecessary, as his stare had caused Sergeant Browne to pause and stand up straight, almost at attention.

Yes, Browne outranked Tommy. He was, as Tommy said, his boss, but the thought of actually pissing Tommy off frightened Sergeant Browne a bit. It was innate; Tommy had that look, for that one moment that just said it all, that "Go ahead and try me" look, and so as Tommy returned to his pad, Sergeant Browne turned and entered his office, closing the door behind him, feeling just slightly less of the man he felt he was just seconds before.

One by one, the rest of the squad filtered in -- Stein first, then Colletti, then Doyle, all shared their good mornings and poured their second or third cups of coffee and began on their morning caseloads.

"Good morning, my lovelies, good morning," Charice Tate, the squad's PAA (Police Administrative Assistant), loudly announced her presence with her ever positive attitude and ear to ear smile.

"Everyone gets two today, and nothing heavy for none of ya'll today either. Was a nice, easy night last night in the old 2-1," she exclaimed, as she dropped two case folders in front of each of the detectives, "But, Detective Keane, Charice do got something special for you, handsome."

"Oh yeah, what you got for me, Charice?" Tommy asked, rather unenthusiastically.

"Last night you got a 877-TIPS call on your missing."

"What? Really? Why didn't anybody call me last night?" he said, considerably more excited than he had been two seconds prior.

"Shoot... I don't know honey. I don't know how half the shit around here gets done at all half the time. But here you go." Charice handed him a printout with some information.

"Thanks, Charice, thank you so much."

"You got it, Detective."

"What is it, Tommy, what's it say?" Doreen came closer.

"Yeah, Tom, what you got there?" Mark Stein asked.

"Name and number of a cab driver, thinks he may have picked up the boy with a woman, the morning of, at John Jay Park." Tommy's excitement grew.

Doreen began to speak, but Tommy put up his hand, to silence her as he dialed the number he was given.

"Hello, hello, is this Jose Mejia? Yes? Okay, this is Detective Keane calling about the tip you called in last night... okay... okay... okay... okay. So you picked them up at John Jay park and then drove them to 96th Street and Lexington, where you think they got on the subway... okay great. Listen my friend, I need to meet you for an interview today. Can you tell me where you are? ... You're working, okay. Can you come here to the precinct?... Yeah, this is the 2-1, you know where it is? ...Okay terrific, what? What? ... Okay 15 to 20 minutes, very good, I'll be waiting for you here. Call me when you arrive and I'll come downstairs and bring you up... Very good, see you then."

"Fuck yeah!" Tommy said, when his conversation was over.

"What's he got, Tommy?" Doyle asked.

"I don't know, but it's something... it's something."

The twenty minutes turned into thirty, then the thirty into forty, as Tommy's patience waned. He picked up his phone to call Jose Mejia back, and just then his phone rang.

"Keane... Glad you called, Jose. I was just going to call you back... No, I know parking is always a nightmare around here. Listen, just pull over into a bus stop or hydrant and wait for me, okay? I'll be right there."

Tommy stood up, "Cab driver is downstairs, Doreen, you wanna come with for this one?" he said as he pulled on his jacket.

"Duh. Yeah, what do you think? Of course I do," was her reply as she too grabbed her jacket from the back of her chair, following Tommy out.

Together they made their way downstairs, Tommy calling Jose Mejia again, as they left the building, "Hey, Jose, where are you?... Okay, cool, thanks."

Tommy motioned with his head to Doreen, "Hydrant on Park" he said. They walked over to Park Avenue, where they found Mr. Mejia leaning against his green cab, parked at a hydrant, with his arms crossed.

Jose Mejia was about five-foot-seven, 130 to 140 pounds, and 37 years old. He wore a denim jacket, with a Dominican flag patch sewn on the left chest, blue denim jeans, a polo shirt, and a grey Scally cap. He had been driving a cab in New York for seventeen years and living in Washington Heights, for the last twenty.

Tommy opened the conversation, "Nice to meet you, Sir, thank you so much for coming to meet us. I'm Detective Keane and this is Detective Doyle," he said, as he reached out his hand to Mr. Mejia's, who took Tommy's and then Doyle's hand for a firm shake.

"Hello... Hello," he replied, as he shook their hands.

"So, Mr. Mejia, Jose, what can you tell us about this fare from John Jay Park and why you called us?"

Jose Mejia began to tell them the story, step by step, calmly and coolly, in a very methodical and detailed manner.

"Yes sirs -- sorry, Sir and Madame -- I picked up a fare at the train station on 125th Street and Park, not at the subway, you know, but by the Metro North station. A very small woman, dressed in a long, black coat and a black hat, she was maybe from the Philippines? I think? She had that look.

"So I take her to 5th Avenue and 85th Street. She says she has to meet someone in the playground there in Central Park and if I can wait, so I say, 'Sure, okay.'

"So she comes back to the cab and then asks me to go to 79th and 5th, where the other playground is. So I say, 'Okay,' and she asks me to wait again.

"So she comes back right, and then asks me to go to John Jay Park, right, you know, Cherokee Place right. And she says... she says, 'Just a minute, wait okay?' So yeah, I says 'Okay,' right, I mean I'm here anyways right? What else I'm gonna do?

"She has me waiting all over town outside these playgrounds, but the meter is running and I can't pick up no street hails here cause I'm a green cab right? So I says 'Yes, sure I will wait.' So like, she gets out right, and walks across the street into the park, and I don't see nothing else.

"But maybe like not even two, maybe three minutes, she opens the door and gets in with a little boy. Dark jacket, maybe blue, maybe grey, I don't know. But he sits down with her right, and she says, 'Take me to 96th Street and Lexington please,' so yeah I say 'Okay' right and I drive them up to 96th Street, where she wants to go, and she pays and gets out right, and she gets in the subway, number 6, going south. That's it right? No, that's not it. So I go back to work. I pick up another fare right, and this nice lady, kinda pretty lady says 'Hey' to me, 'Someone left a toy back here. Did you have a child in here?'"

Jose Mejia paused to take a breath and scratch at his hairline under his cap, then returned to his narrative.

"I says 'Yes' right? Because I did, right? So I drop her off, and she pays me and gives me this toy through the window, right?

"I don't think of this at all, nothing. I just finish my shift, and when I leave the car, I take the toy with me. It's a nice toy, maybe I give it to my niece, right?

"So, next day I pick up the car again and I work all day. I don't think about nothing, no toy, no lady, no nothing, and I have a pretty good day. But I'm having some dinner, at dinner time right? And the news on the Telemundo says just a little thing about this boy, that you are looking for him right? I'm in the restaurant and just for a second, I see this little short thing on the news, on the TV right? And I says, 'Oh man, oh man, I bet that is me.' Maybe that is me and that lady, it has to be, who else would it be right? So, I call the 877-TIPS number, and you call me this morning, and I come and meet you, and here we are now and I am telling you right?"

Tommy asked, "Was the boy upset? Was he crying?"

Jose continued, "No… nothing, like nothing. Just normal, sitting with the lady in the back right. She was talking nice to him, and he was talking nice back to her, you know? Like perfectly normal, right."

"And what were they talking about?"

"Nothing I could hear. You know there's the divide, with Plexiglass, and they had little voices right. Even when the lady told me where she wanted to go, I had to ask again, cause she was a quiet lady."

"Did you log these fares?"

"Yes, Sir, I always log everything, Sir, just like I am supposed to. I have them here, do you like to see them?"

"Yes, please," Tommy said.

Jose reached into the open window and pulled out his log, "Here, here you go, Detective."

"Thank you," Tommy replied, and he took photos of the page with his phone, then handed it back, and asked, "What can you tell me about this toy the woman gave you?"

Jose reached into the window again, turned and handed Tommy a brown stuffed rabbit.

"Here, this is the toy the woman gave, this toy bunny rabbit."

Both Tommy and Doreen's hearts stopped for a moment. They made eye contact with one another, then returned their attention back to Jose. This was Hayden's stuffed rabbit, and they knew it. Tommy took the soft plush toy in his left hand and again shook Jose's hand firmly with his right.

"Mr. Mejia… Jose, you have helped us out in a big way today. Thank you very much. Listen, this is my card. If you have any more information, please give me a call. I may be calling you back also, and thank you. Thank you so very much for helping us out with this. It means so much, you coming forward."

"Yes, Sir, thank you too. I hope you find this boy, I hope he is okay." And with that Jose again shook hands with both Tommy and Doreen, then got back in his cab, waved to the detectives, and went back to work.

Both detectives stood silent for a moment as Jose Mejia drove off. They looked down at the brown bunny rabbit, then at one another. A huge break in the case -- maybe, hopefully yes -- but they also held something personal of little Hayden's in their hands. If it was possible at all for this case to become even more real to Tommy and Doreen, it just did.

"She was hunting," Tommy said softly.

"Hunting?" Doreen asked.

"Yes, she went from playground to playground, looking for a kid she could snatch."

"Wow, yeah it looks that way, doesn't it?"

Both detectives paused for a moment as they took Tommy's revelation in.

"What next, Tommy?" Doreen asked.

"What next, what next?" Tommy replied, and paused for a moment.

"96th Street, southbound, number six. Maybe we can catch her on camera there, and if we are lucky, we can catch her getting off somewhere later."

"Let's go," Doreen replied.

***

Tommy and Doreen drove up to the IRT number 6, southbound subway station, on the southwest corner of the intersection of 96th Street and Lexington Avenue. They parked their Crown Vic in the bus stop, in front of the entrance.

They made their way down the stairs and to the attendant, who sat inside the bulletproof token booth. They identified themselves and asked about any surveillance cameras that may exist in the station, and if they could see any footage from three days ago.

The young woman, who was working the booth at the time, said she couldn't help them, but put a call into a supervisor who would be there soon.

Tommy and Doreen walked to the wall to wait for the supervisor, and watched the parade of commuters coming and going.

Approximately 40 minutes had passed, when a Miss Tanisha Miles came walking down the stairs into the station.

"Hello, hello," she greeted both detectives, "You detectives need to see some of our cameras?"

"Yes, please," Tommy replied.

"Please, please follow me," Ms. Miles said, in a very upbeat, happy to help way, as she led them to a control room on the platform. She sat in a chair, in front of a desk and a monitor, typed in her code, and asked for the day, date, and time in question.

Tommy gave the information and Tanisha Miles queued up the video. "What are you looking for exactly, Detectives? I'll fast forward and see what we can find for you."

"We have a very small woman, in a black coat and hat, who ran off with a little boy, in a grey jacket, and--"

"No... that little boy that got snatched from the park the other day? That little boy?" She stopped looking at the

- 131 -

computer and swung her head around to look up at the detectives, with her mouth aghast.

"Yes, ma'am, that's the one. So you heard?"

"Hell yeah I heard. Got an Amber Alert text on my phone. Okay let's see if we can find this bitch," Tanisha Miles said, with a little anger and determination, as she swung back to the monitor, the beads on her braids knocking together. "Okay, okay, here we go now," she mumbled to herself, as she began running through the video.

"Ha! There you go! That who you're looking for, Detectives?"

"Yes, ma'am, that is exactly who we are looking for, Miss Miles," Tommy replied, with a smile.

There were five cameras in this particular station, and only three of them were operational at the time, but they clearly showed little Hayden Marshall being led down the stairs, hand in hand, with a small woman in a black coat and hat, wearing sunglasses and carrying a blue tote bag. They went through the turnstiles and onto the platform, where they both sat on a bench, and then boarded the next arriving train.

"Okay… So we have them here. How do we find where they get off?" Doreen asked.

"Well, I can send you down to the main control room downtown and they will be able to help you… But you got me right now, Detectives. If you like, we can just go station to station, and see where this bitch gets off?"

"We can do that?" Tommy asked.

"Hell yeah! I'm here, I got the keys and the authority, and besides, I wanna see where this goes," Tanisha Miles replied.

"Okay then, next stop 86th Street," Tommy said.

"Yes, Sir. We'll take two cars, then we won't have to drive nobody back here," Tanisha replied.

As they left, Tanisha Miles waved to the attendant on duty. They climbed the stairs, and the three of them got into their respective cars, both of which were parked next to one another in the bus stop outside of the station, and made their way to the next stop, 86th Street and Lexington Avenue.

Again, both cars parked in the bus stop outside of the subway entrance, and made their way down the stairs. Tanisha Miles waved at the attendant on duty and led the detectives to the control room. She again sat in front of a desk and a monitor, and queued the video to the day, date, and time. She raced through it, fairly quickly, and then reversed it.

"Look! Look here, that's them... That's them, but they changed clothes. You see that? That's them, but she's in a different coat, and he is too!"

"God bless you, Tanisha. You found them, didn't you," replied Tommy.

Tanisha Miles, Tommy, and Doreen were all thrilled. One stop away and, bang, they had found little Hayden and his abductor leaving the station, but now wearing different clothing. The woman was now in a long, white coat and wearing a red hat, and little Hayden was in a new red jacket and had no hat at all. Together they walked out of the 86th Street subway station.

The thrill soon left all of them, though, as the reality set in that they still had a little boy to find.

"Give me one of y'all's cards, and I will make sure I get some copies of this to your precinct by the end of the day," Tanisha Miles said.

"Thank you so very, very much, Miss Miles. You have helped us out so much today," Tommy replied.

"Yes, thank you," said Doreen.

"Don't thank me, Detectives. You go find that boy now, please."

"Yes, indeed," Tommy replied.

***

Tommy and Doreen left the subway station and began their canvas of the storefronts on Lexington Avenue. They asked shop owners who had surveillance cameras if they could review their tapes. Again, they struck gold, as many of the shops along Lexington did have cameras. Block by block, they were able to follow little Hayden and his abductor, heading southbound on the west side of Lexington Avenue all the way to 82nd Street, where again they disappeared.

Not finding them on any of the cameras south of 82nd Street, they headed west on 82nd Street, towards Park Avenue. There they were able to find three working cameras, facing the street, but no footage of the couple.

They then headed east, all the way to Third Avenue, where they found four cameras facing the street, but again none with any footage. By the time they had finished their fruitless search, and interviews in every direction of the intersection of 82nd Street and Lexington Avenue, their tour had ended, and they were now 90 minutes into overtime. Once again, they headed back to the precinct without finding little Hayden. But this time they had a bit of hope that he was still alive.

***

Tommy and Doreen returned to the station house and despite a nice break in the case, Tommy found himself lost again... 82nd Street? All leads end at 82nd Street. Doreen ran everything she could on every address on the block, through the computer at the precinct, but there was nothing they found that they could sink their teeth into. Nothing that was worth anything, as far as a clue, or suspect of any kind.

Every little bit of video footage they could find, south of 82nd Street and Lexington, west of 82nd and Lexington, over to Park, and east all the way down and across Third Avenue, there was nothing. Nothing. Not one other image of little Hayden Jon, or his very small abductor.

Tommy and Doreen had conducted a canvas of the area. They knocked on every door, and spoke to every doorman they could, on 82nd Street between Park Avenue and Third Avenue, and were able to find video footage from a total of seven different buildings all facing the street that should have been able to catch something of the two of them.

But no, nothing. Where did they go?

"They didn't just vanish," Tommy said to Doreen.

"Do you think they caught another cab? It's possible she hailed a cab on the corner and then again they just disappeared?" Doreen asked in reply.

"It's possible, Doreen. She's turning out to be a crafty little thing, with all this backtracking and clothes changing… They may have hopped into another cab. They also could be in one of the ten or twelve buildings that have no surveillance on them, in any direction right off any one of the four corners there… Think, Tommy think, how can we find this kid? Where can he be?"

"What can we do here, Tommy, what's next? The computers are giving me nothing here, as far as any red flags on any of these buildings. Not a single suspicious person or criminal history of any kind is coming up for any address on either of these blocks."

"I know, Doreen, I know. We just have to look deeper. How? That's the question… I think. I don't know, I think we are done for today though. I don't know where else we could go right now. I think we will have to start this up again tomorrow."

"Yeah, I think you're right, Tommy. I'm burnt to a crisp today, I need some fresh eyes for this, and tomorrow I'll be ready to dive back in."

"Yup, you and I both. We hit yet another wall here. Let's both think on how we can get over it. Let's head home."

Chapter Eight

Tommy's desperation in finding little Hayden was becoming more extreme with each day that passed. This was now the end of the third day of the investigation, the day he was supposed to forward it to the Missing Persons squad. That was the protocol, but he had finally got a break and there was no way he was letting it go, not just yet. He needed to follow this. He desperately needed to find this boy.

But where would this break lead? Or was this it? Did the trail end here? Did this woman get into another cab? She had proven herself to be an exceedingly careful and crafty kidnapper. Where did she take this boy? What was her intent? Was little Hayden still alive?

***

Tommy started the walk home, back to his mother's, as he usually did. Only on this night he took Lexington Avenue north. As he approached 81st Street, he slowed his pace, and took note of every shop, every building, and every vestibule approaching 82nd Street.

The streets were very quiet, almost completely empty. As he neared 82nd Street, Tommy would stop at every doorway for a few seconds, and study them. He looked up at the windows, stood still and turned around in circles scanning everything, taking a mental note of what he saw. If anyone had been watching him, they would have sworn he was out of his mind, drunk, or on drugs. But it was a process, he had to just take it all in, and he was happy to be one of very few people out on that intersection at that time, so there were next to no distractions.

'Where did you go, little Hayden? Where did that little woman take you? Did the two of you hop into another cab here on the corner? Or are you here? Can you be here somewhere, somewhere just yards away waiting for me? Oh Hayden, please, please please please be alive. Please know I'm looking for you.'

Tommy reached into his pocket and pulled out his cell phone. He searched out the number to Reif's Tavern, paused for a second, and then hit the button.

"Reif's," a man on the other end answered.

"Hey, how you doing? This is Tommy calling for Terry. Can you put him on, please?"

"There's no one named Terry here, pal. In fact I don't know no Terry at all." And then the phone hung up.

Tommy took a breath and then called back.

"Reif's."

"Hey, if Terry is there, tell him Tommy Keane is looking for him. And if he's not there, tell him Tommy Keane is looking for him, thanks," and then Tommy hung up the phone and started walking north again, on Lexington Avenue.

Tommy didn't make it the four blocks to 86th Street before his phone went off. It was from a number he didn't recognize.

"Keane," he answered.

"Hello, sweetheart, how you doin? You missing me?" It was his lifelong friend, and underworld figure, Terry Callahan.

"Hey, Terry, how you doing? You around? I need to ask you about something."

"I'm not right now, but I can be real soon. What do you need and where do you want to meet?"

"I just need a couple of minutes, and anywhere you like, I'm calling you. I'd like someplace quiet though, even a quick street meet."

"Okay, where are you at right now?"

"86th and Lex."

"You wanna just keep walking north? I'll head up to Lex and we'll meet on 92nd Street by the Y, is that cool? And how cold is it out?"

"Yeah, that's perfect, and actually it's not too bad at all, maybe 40 degrees. What you afraid of the cold now, Terry?"

"No, I just need to know what to put on, dummy. Okay, thanks, I'll see you in a few."

"Cool, Terry, thanks."

***

As Tommy approached 92nd Street, he could see Terry leaning against the building on the corner. His silhouette gave him away. From over a block away Terry was recognizable, even his shadowy image under the streetlight exuded confidence.

Terry wore a similar leather car coat to the one Tommy wore. But rather than the sports coat, shirt, tie, slacks, and Oxfords that Tommy wore for work, Terry stood waiting in the decidedly more comfortable black pullover crew neck sweatshirt, Levi's, which he wore with a two inch cuff, and shell-toed Adidas Superstars on his feet.

As Tommy approached, they made eye contact. Terry stood and waited until Tommy met him on the corner and they both engaged in a long and hard hug, their leather coats crunching and squeaking against one another.

"I miss you, brother," Terry said softly.

"And I miss you, my friend."

"So, what can I do for you, brother? I know you wouldn't be reaching out to me if it wasn't important."

"It's pretty important alright," Tommy replied, "I have this missing three year old--"

"The one from John Jay Park?" Terry interrupted.

"Yeah, that's the one... So you heard?"

"Of course. I hear everything. We even have some eyes and ears out in the streets ourselves, looking to see if we find anything out about this kid."

"Good man. Thank you."

"No need for thanks, it's what we do."

"I know, I know. So listen, we found out this kid was abducted. He was abducted by a very small woman, possibly Filipino? We're not sure, but she is a very small woman. We have a cabby, he picked her up at 125th Street drove her to 85th and Fifth, then 79th and Fifth, and then John Jay Park, where she snatched this boy. He then took her up to 96th Street, where she got on the southbound train, with the boy, to 86th Street. From there, she shows up on camera, coming out of the subway, her and the boy wearing different colored clothing then they had gotten on the train with, and then they walk south on Lexington to 82nd Street, where they vanish. And that's it, we got nothing after that."

"They changed clothes... huh. She's a sneaky little thing, ain't she? All this uptown downtown shit, and then she changes clothes on the train, just in case you do catch her on video. She's clever."

"Yeah, very clever. But we got her. Down to 82nd Street anyway, then they disappear again. What I want to ask you, is if you know anyone down there? Maybe a 32B guy (doorman)? Any of the business owners, anyone in the vicinity of 82nd and Lex that might maybe know something?"

Terry paused for a moment. "You know I don't like to go south of 86th Street, Tommy, but you know what? I got just the guy you want to talk to. His name is Rudy... Rudy Barr. He's a super on 82nd and Third. Tall Panamanian guy, good guy, but a bad gambler. He knows everything about everyone over in that area. He's been the super in that building for over thirty years at least. And you'll like him. He's a real decent guy, overall."

"Really? Ahh that's fucking awesome, Terry. This guy, Rudy, do you got anything on him? Does he owe you anything?"

"Nope, nothing, not at the moment anyway. But he'd certainly like to have some points with me I'm sure, and with you as well. Listen, I'll get word to him that you're coming to see him... Tomorrow good?"

"Yeah, tomorrow is great."

"Okay, cool, I don't know the number of his building but it's the last one on the block, on the northwest corner. He also frequents the Mad River Pub on Third as well. Like I said, he's a decent guy, you'll have no trouble with him."

"Thank you, Terry. Thank you so much."

"Hey, let's just hope he can help you a little. How's everything else? You alright? You're looking a little beat up today, pal. Caitlin? Cookie? Your Moms?"

"I'm alright, Terry, other than this missing kid. This kid is eating at me, he's been missing for three days, and that is not good, not good at all. Thank god we found the video of this woman and were able to track them to 82nd Street at least, but again it's been three days and I'm just hoping we're not too late."

"I don't envy you, pal. Listen, you know you have my support. Anything I can do to help, please let us know. This kid is lucky to have you on the case, Tommy. If anyone can find this kid Tommy Keane can."

"Thanks for the kind words, Terry, but I have to tell you this one is shaking me a little. I'm trying my best to stay on top of it, but the worst keeps creeping into my head."

"Well, don't let it!" Terry said firmly, "You need to stay clear headed and strong for this kid, Tommy... You know that. Stay on top of it and find this kid and the monster that ran off with him."

"I know, Terry, I know."

"So how's everything else? Caitlin? Cookie? Your Moms?"

"Things are good. The girls are good, thanks. I'm going to go up and see Caitlin, up at Cookie's. She'll be home for Thanksgiving on Wednesday, haven't seen her since she went off to school. She's got a new boyfriend she's bringing with her, so that will be interesting."

"Uh oh, a new boyfriend. Well you let me know if you don't like him, Tommy, and we'll have his ass in plastic bags the day after."

They both laughed.

"I'm sure he's a good kid. She's a smart girl, my Caitlin is, I really don't worry at all for her, Terry."

"Yeah, she's a smart one, way smarter than either one of us, that's for sure."

"And you? What you have going on this week?

"Sissy and I are going to give out the turkeys, then we're just going to go out to dinner... it's what we usually do. You know she don't cook, and really, neither of us like either of our families, so, we just make the rounds, give out the birds, and then go have a quiet dinner, just the two of us."

Every Thanksgiving morning, Terry and his crew, would give out as many as a hundred turkeys to needy and elderly people in the neighborhood. It was a way to help buy love and loyalty. Although he never seemed to catch on, and over the years no one ever had the balls to tell him, that a 12 to 15 pound frozen turkey takes three or four days to thaw out. So handing them out frozen on Thanksgiving day really did no one a Thanksgiving favor. But the sentiment was there, regardless, and respect and loyalty returned on behalf of the neighborhood's lower class.

"You're a good guy, Terry. Listen… I love you. Say hello to Sissy, and give her my love, please."

They hugged again.

"You too, Tommy. Take care, and please, if you need any more help with this kid, or anything else, you know you can always give me a call."

"Yes sir, I do. Thanks again. I do have one more thing to ask, Terry."

"Yeah? What's that?"

"You guys want a dog? I got a puppy, a Boston Terrier puppy, I need to find a home for. He's really a good little--"

"Ha! No, I don't want no dog. I had a dog, and he died, I'm never going through that shit again, that fucker broke my heart."

"You sure, Terry? He's a really cool little dog, perfect for an apartment. I'm sure Sissy--"

"No. No dogs, Tommy, I can't stand to lose them when they go. Happy Thanksgiving to you and yours, and say hello to your mother for me, please."

Once again, they embraced, and Tommy turned and headed south on Lexington. Terry paused for a moment as he watched his lifelong friend walk away down the Avenue. The man he loved and trusted above all others was now separated from him, separated by the side of the law they both stood on. Terry sighed a sigh of despair, and then he began his way back towards the projects, east on 92nd Street.

Hayden Jon Marshall

Chapter Nine

Tuesday, 10:12 AM - 173 East 82nd Street

Tommy parked in front of the fire hydrant just a few feet from the building. 173 East 82nd Street was a large, ten-story building, built in 1968. It ran for the entire block on Third Avenue. The building included 100 one-to-three bedroom apartments, and had six storefronts on Third Avenue, one of which was a supermarket that took up half the block.

Tommy entered the building, where he saw the same doorman on duty he had seen the day before, as he and Doreen had been canvasing the block. They had interviewed everyone they could, including this man, who stood behind the tall desk in the lobby.

"Morning, Detective. Back again? What can I do for you today?" The short, round, Puerto Rican doorman said, with a smile.

"Hey, how you doing, pal. I'm looking for the super, he around? Rudy? Rudy Barr?"

"Yeah, he's somewhere. Let me see if I can get a hold of him for you."

The doorman picked up a small walkie talkie, pressed a button and spoke into it, "Rudy... Rudy, come to the door. I have a detective from the 21st here for you."

"Okay, baybay," was the audible response from the super on the other end.

"He's on his way," the doorman said.

Rudy Barr came walking out of a door located to the side of the lobby. Rudy was 70 years old, but could have easily passed for 50. He was a tall, dark-skinned, handsome man with short cropped, salt and pepper hair and a broad, bright white smile. He was dressed from top to bottom in navy Dickies workwear, with "Rudy" embroidered in script on the right chest of his jacket, and 173 E 82 on the left, in red thread. Rudy walked quickly and with purpose. He spoke with a Panamanian/Spanish accent, but also in a way that sounded as though he learned English from some 1960's beatnik rock and rollers. His speech was lively, entertaining, and just plain fun to listen to.

"Heyy, Detective! Nice to meet you, man. I hear so much good tings about you man, I read you in the paper many times also, you a busy man, baybay (baby)."

Before Tommy could even respond, Rudy was talking to the doorman behind the desk, beside where the two of them stood in the lobby.

"Ernie, dis is Detective Keane, ooh, him da real deal baybay. I know him from da papers man, him no joke, him serious business, baybay, dat I tell you."

Turning his attention back to Tommy, Rudy asked, "What can I do for you, Detective Keane? My friend, my friend, him tells me I can help you out maybe, man if I can help you, baybay, you know I will, man. You just ask me what you need, man."

Tommy smiled to himself; he immediately liked everything about Mr. Rudy Barr.

"Yes, Sir, I'm hoping you can. Let's step outside here, for a moment."

"Yes, Sir, of course, of course. Let's step outside here, man."

Tommy walked outside, leaned up against a car parked in the street, and began.

"We are looking for a missing child, a little three year-old boy. He went missing four days ago from John Jay Park and the last time he was seen was right up on the corner over there on Lexington Avenue. Then poof, he was gone. He was in the company of a very small woman, who appears to be possibly Filipino, maybe Hispanic?"

"Yeah, yeah man. Me heard about dis little man going missing at da park man, me get the text on me phone... You know dat alert ... Yeah, yeah, me hear dat."

"Well, our friend Terry seems to think you know everything that goes on on this block, says you've been the eyes and ears around here for almost thirty years."

"Try tirty six, tirty six years I work dis building, baybay. And yes, me see everyting on dis block, and you say, you say ...little woman? Very small little woman, look like maybe a Fillipino, yes? Me tinks me can help you, Detective. Me don't know nutting about no little boy, but we do have a very small woman who do live, or maybe her work, I don't know, live, maybe work, here on dis block."

"Really?" Tommy was excited, "Tell me, please, what do you know?"

"Me know me see her, dats all I know… Me see her once in da while, not too much, not too often. Me just see her, for many years her will walk by here. I say her maybe 50 years old, maybe? Very small woman, and yes, me tink maybe could be Filipino, you notice her because she is small, not a midget, just very small. And her always seem to come down da block, mostly on dat side of da street, just go back and forth, from up da block… Here, come up da block with me, Detective, I show you what maybe me tink man."

Tommy and Rudy walked up the quiet, tree-lined street toward Lexington Avenue. About three buildings shy of the corner, Rudy stopped.

"Me not so sure, Detective, but, me tinks maybe dis woman, maybe her comes from one of dem tree houses across da street, there."

He pointed to three identical brick row houses that stood side by side. All were very nice, small, single family homes, about 50 feet off of Lexington Avenue on the south side of the street. Two of the buildings were red brick, and were next to another one, the first one coming from Lexington Avenue, which was painted black. Each building was three stories high, with a small, two-step stoop at its entrance. Other than a few different flower pots, ornamental window boxes, window coverings, and the one being painted black, they looked exactly the same.

"I don't know, man. Me tinks, maybe one of dese small buildings, and me don't know why? Maybe, maybe one time me see her coming in or out?" Rudy said, shrugging his shoulders and holding his hands up with his palms facing up. "Dis, I can't tell you, Detective, all me say is maybe one of dese, and just maybe because me maybe tink so, man. Sorry baybay, me don't know no more than that. But yes, if you want a very small, Filipino woman, we got one of dem on dis block, man."

"Mr. Barr? My friend, you have helped me out more than you know. Thank you very much," Tommy replied, as he stuck out his hand, and shook Rudy's vigorously, "Please, let's head back down to your building."

As they walked back down the block, Tommy removed a card from his pocket and handed it to Rudy, "If ever I can help you out, or if you see, hear, or think of anything else I may want to know, please call me anytime, day or night, on my cell here. And thank you again, Rudy, you've been a big help today."

"No problem, man, if you tink you need more from me, please do ask, Detective. Me do anyting to help you out man."

"Thanks, Rudy, I appreciate it. Hey, you wouldn't be in the market for a puppy, would you?"

"A dog? Yeah man, me would love a dog! No can do though, baybay. Management don't allow it here, tenants can have dem, but employees? No way man, not allowed."

"Really? Well, that doesn't seem fair."

"No, me wanted a dog for a long time too, but managements says no."

They shook hands again and then Tommy headed back up the block and took a seat on the stoop of one of the buildings opposite the three buildings Rudy had pointed out. He took out his notebook and wrote down the addresses, and studied them for about an hour, waiting to see if there was any kind of action at all. There wasn't.

These were older, probably pre-Civil War era homes, and although they were small, this was now a very expensive neighborhood. These homes were no doubt worth millions. Tommy, realizing his scrutiny was proving fruitless, hopped up and quickly headed back to the car. He drove back to the precinct, so he could run these buildings in the computer and see what it might reveal.

Upon returning to the station house, Tommy was spotted by Captain Peleggi, who called to him as he approached the steps leading to the second floor.

"Keane! Detective Keane, what can you tell me about that Gillstone case? Can we be expecting an arrest soon? I want that case closed soon, Detective!"

"Yes, Sir, Captain. I have a lead and hope to be closing that case soon," Tommy replied, knowing he had absolutely nothing. Since the disappearance of Hayden Marshall the very morning he received the Gillstone case, he hadn't even considered another of his cases for investigation. But he said what he had to say to get up the stairs.

"Very good, Detective. Know I am paying attention to that one!"

"Yes, Sir, it's noted," Tommy replied as he made his way up the stairs, 'Missing three-year-old and this political cunt is worried about some rich bitch's earrings,' Tommy thought to himself.

Tommy sat in front of the computer and searched the three addresses on 82nd Street. The first was owned by a Herbert Abramson, who had resided there since 1988. A further search of Mister Abramson showed he was, or at least was once, a very wealthy investor and trader on Wall Street, no criminal record, no marriage records, really nothing.

The building next door was purchased by a Mr. and Mrs. Rodger Wilkinson in 1996, and a further search showed them both to be from England. He was also in finance, and neither had criminal records.

The third building was owned by a Mr. Adrian Greenspan who was involved in the importing and exporting of wines from Italy. He was married to an Italian man named Mario Batiolo, and they also had no criminal records.

'Fucking computer… C'mon, give me something I can bite into.'

Tommy continued to bang away at the computer, but nothing illicit or suspicious revealed itself in regards to any of these locations.

***

Meanwhile, back on 88th Street, Roya's tens of hours of work suddenly paid off. While she was making a new pot of coffee, both of her Brute Force attacks on Derek Spree broke into his private little world.

Roya returned to her room with her large, hot cup of black coffee, expecting nothing. She glanced at her monitors and was thrilled, more than thrilled. There it was, waiting for her. Both desktop screens had dramatically changed.

A large female smiley face emoji, with a bow on its head, and the caption, "You Are In!!!" was waiting for her on the computer to the left, and a large male smiley face on the right side popped up with the caption, "Hells Yeah Bruh!!"

She was in! She placed her cup of coffee to the side and sat down. Now the next phase of the action -- the searching. Roya had gained access to his system, now she had to search it and with a new, strong, (and very excited) second wind, she did.

Roya didn't have to spend hours searching once she got into Derek Spree's private world. It may have taken tens of hours, and three computers working nonstop, to break into his system, but once inside his well-guarded cocoon of crime, Roya was almost disappointed at how open and sloppy Derek Spree was. She fully expected additional layers, and coded password-protected files, but, no. Once she was in, she was in.

Derek Spree had dozens of galleries of little girls. Some were no more than random photos of little girls. Most all of them appeared to be around the age of ten to twelve. Most were white, but there were some of every ethnicity. The vast majority of these were clothed photos, some semi-nude, and occasionally, fully nude.

Then, there were some that looked like photoshoots. These collections were named; nothing more than a first name, unless there were two girls with the same name. For instance there were three Anna's, listed as Anna 1, Anna 2, and Anna 3. Many of these girls appeared to be foreign. His favorites, or maybe just the most prevalent, appeared to be Eastern European. Roya decided this herself, because most were white but still had a somewhat exotic, or unusual beauty to them that seemed less typical of American girls. Then of course, there were a few obvious signs, a children's book, or a can of Coca Cola. With a second look, only "Coca Cola" was recognizable, the rest of the words on the can were in a foreign language. Most had odd letters that Roya believed to be Russian or Ukrainian -- both nations use variations of the Cyrillic Script, something Roya knew nothing about, but was able to recognize right away.

She continued to search through Spree's files. Another set of folders she found were much more disturbing, and although they were impossible to look at, Roya looked at each and every one. At this point, she had become obsessed. These folders were labeled by location. They, in essence, were Derek Spree's vacation albums:

Bangkok

Puerto Vallarta

Phuket 1

Phuket 2

DR (which she believed to be Dominican Republic)

Grenada

Richmond VA 1-3

And Matamoros PA 1-9

Within each of these folders, there were multiple photos of one man -- or sometimes two men, in the case of the Matamoros files -- having sex with children. Horrid shots of these little girls, dressed in what appeared to be brand new little outfits. Sundresses, and matching skirt and shirt sets with little flowers on them, seemed to be the favorite choice of attire for these photos. These were followed by photos of children in various stages of undress, catalogued almost like a strip tease, and then followed by actual sex acts. They always featured the one man she assumed was Derek Spree. But occasionally there were photos of another man taking part. On four occasions, both men with a single girl. Every sex act imaginable was chronicled in these files.

Some of the girls were visibly shaken and crying from fear, and from obvious pain. Others though, showed no emotion at all. They just stared into the camera with dead eyes, and somehow these little girls affected Roya the most.

Stoically, Roya went through every album and every folder contained in every file she found. Without emotion, as if she were a professional, seasoned investigator.

And when she was done, she sat back, drank down about half of a bottle of water she had opened a while before, and then began to cry. She cried so hard that it turned into audible sobbing, so she stood up and lay face down on her bed, with her face in her pillow, in fear that her mother might hear her and come knocking at her door.

This sobbing lasted for quite some time, possibly a full 20 or 30 minutes, before she was completely cried out. She then got up, wiped her face, and went back to work. She downloaded everything she had discovered about Mr. Derek Spree onto two separate Duo Plus flash drives.

She then went to the mirror. "My god, you look like shit," she said out loud to her reflection, wiping her bloodshot eyes with her hands and looking at herself for the first time in two days. Her hair was an unkempt mess. Her eyes bloodshot with black circles underneath them from lack of sleep. She shook her head at her appearance and then lifted the bottom of her t-shirt up and re-wiped her eyes, then the snot from her runny nose. Roya then returned to her bed, sat down, inhaled deeply, exhaled, and picked up her cell phone and called Tommy.

Instead of his usual, "Keane," Tommy recognized the number and answered, "Roya, how you doing, kid?"

Roya had to take a breath, "I made the hack, Tommy… and I…" her voice began to crack, "He's a bad guy, Tommy."

Tommy could hear Roya was in distress. "You alright, kid?" Tommy asked, as he heard Roya's sobs, "Roya… You okay?" he asked in a lower, more comforting, voice.

"No, Tommy. I'm pretty fucking far from okay," she answered in a decidedly more confident and somewhat angry tone, "So, what's next?" she asked.

"Well, hang on to what you got. I want to see it, confirm it is indeed Spree. Then, well, you and I can't do anything with it ourselves, but I'll forward it to the Special Victims unit. I know a couple of really decent guys down there. I'll have to do it anonymously, but that's what we'll do… Is it, is it very bad, Roya?" Tommy asked again, in as comforting a tone as he could.

"It's the worst," Roya said, rubbing her hand over her forehead, trying to erase the images.

"Okay, kid. Okay, listen, try to take it easy, I'm going to come see you as soon as I can. Where are you?"

"I'm home, but you can't come here. My mother is here, and I don't want her knowing anything."

"Okay, do you want to go to a restaurant or the diner?"

"Really, Tommy, I'd like to go for a drink. Can we go for a drink, Tommy?"

"Absolutely, Roya. Just give me a bit. I'll call you as soon as I can."

"Thanks, Tommy."

"And Roya… You did good, kid."

"I know," Roya replied, as she began to cry again.

***

Tommy called Roya the second he was free, "Hey, Roya, how you doing? You a bit better?"

"Yeah, I guess, better. I don't know, but I've got my emotions in check, let's just say that."

"I understand. I'm going to be heading uptown now, do you still want to go for that drink?"

"It's all I've been thinking of, Tommy," Roya replied.

"Okay, where would you like to go?"

"I don't care, somewhere quiet and in the neighborhood. Anywhere is fine, somewhere we can just sit and have a drink, alone and in peace."

"Okay, you want me to come pick you up at the building?"

"No, no, I don't want to hear anything from my mother about any of this, or about why I'm seeing you, or about anything at all. Tell me where you want to go and I'll meet you there."

"Alright... Do you know Nash's -- I mean Bailey's, Baileys Corner? It's on 85th and York, across from Arturo's Restaurant. Do you know it?"

"Yeah, I know where that place is. When do you want to meet?"

"I'm free, and I'll head up there now. Does that work for you?"

"Sure, give me a half an hour, okay? I'll meet you there."

"Very good, kid, I'll see you there."

***

Tommy caught a cab up to Bailey's Corner Pub. He wanted to be sure he was there to meet Roya as soon as she got there. He was unhappy to know that what she had seen had upset her. He always knew, of course, that if they were to gain access to Derek Spree's computer and its inner files and uncover any criminal activity, it would surely be disturbing. He also knew Roya knew this, but he was still hurt, and unhappy with himself, to know it was he who had asked her to help him. It was he, in the end, that got her involved. Regardless of the fact that she volunteered to help Tommy, and almost demanded to take this task on herself, he still bore responsibility for involving her at all. And for that he would always be sorry.

Tommy walked into the pub and saw both Jack and Molly behind the bar. It wasn't particularly busy in the place; the bar side was full, but the tables and chairs to the right were all open but for a foursome who sat towards the back of the pub.

Tommy made eye contact with Jack. "Tommy, how goes it!" he shouted out, as he served a couple towards the near end of the bar. Seconds later, he handed a cold Budweiser and a rocks glass with a double shot of Jameson in it, across the bar to Tommy.

"Hey, Jacky Boy, how you doing today?"

"Better than most, Tommy, better than most," Jack grinned.

Tommy handed him a twenty and then turned and headed over to the front corner of the pub, where he grabbed the empty table in the corner near the windows. As he took off his coat, two small arms wrapped around his waist and gave him a tight squeeze from behind. For a split second it startled him, but as the arms grabbed him, he heard a young woman's voice.

"Tommy, where have you been? I haven't seen you for weeks and I missed ya, big fella."

It was Molly, who had run from behind the bar and grabbed Tommy, quite forcefully, from behind.

Tommy turned, and Molly gave him another hug, burying her head in his chest, "Molly, my love, how you doing, kid?"

"I'm much better now that you're here, Tommy. We've missed you, where have you been?"

"I've been around, Molly. I must have just missed you on your shifts."

"Well, shame on you! You need to pay more attention to my schedule, and make it a point to come see me once or twice a week, or I may start getting Tommy withdrawals...Are you sitting? I'm getting off now, can I come have a drink with you?"

"You know, Molly, I would love that, but I have to say no, I'm meeting someone here in a minute, and we need, well we need to be alone for a bit, kid... I'm sorry."

"No, no sorrys needed, Tommy, I understand. Was good to see you tonight though, come back soon when I'm working okay? I did miss you the last couple weeks," the shine in Molly's eyes dimmed a bit.

"Yeah, of course Molly, I'll be in. You ain't getting rid of me anytime soon," Tommy smiled at her.

"Okay, great," Molly replied, and walked back to the far end of the bar, as Tommy sat in the corner and awaited Roya's arrival.

Roya arrived about fifteen minutes after Tommy had, and pretty much exactly to the half hour she said it would take her. As she entered the pub, she immediately saw Tommy and walked straight over to him. He stood up, and she quickly threw her arms around him and gave him a strong, tight hug, one that she held much longer than a typical greeting. She then stepped back and said hello.

Her eyes were no longer bloodshot. She had taken a shower, brushed her teeth and her hair, and was dressed in a similar style to what she wore the other day when they met in the morning, before work. She had on a black denim jacket, red zip hoodie, and red converse. When she removed her jacket and hoodie, before taking her seat, she revealed the black Airborne Toxic Event band t-shirt she had on underneath, with a gold yellow moon and a crow on it.

"Cool shirt, I like those guys," Tommy said.

"You always had good taste in music, Tommy," Roya replied. She looked good, but her voice had a tone to it, and her face a look, that said she was still distressed over what she had found.

"What can I get you to drink, Roya?" Tommy asked.

"I'll take a Tito's with soda, and a splash of lime, please. And Tommy, can I have a tall one, in a pint glass, please?"

"You got it."

Tommy went back to the bar, and asked Jack for the Tito's and another Budweiser, then returned to the table with the drinks.

"So what? I guess we get right into it, yes?" Roya asked.

"Yeah, if you're ready. When you're ready."

"Okay, yeah, let's just do this and get it over with. Here, here is everything I have," and she handed Tommy one of the USB flash drives, "It's for you to send to your friends at Special Victims… Now, here is what you need to see."

She stood up, and moved her chair, from across the table to next to Tommy, pulled a tablet out of her bag and turned it on. She then began to show Tommy photos of the two men with the girls from some of the files marked "Matamoros PA."

The first photo was of two smiling men, two average-looking white men, both in polo shirts, one with his arm around the other, next to a stone fireplace, both holding Heinekens up to the camera.

"Is either of these men the one you are looking for?" Roya asked.

"Yes, definitely. That's Spree, on the left," Tommy replied.

"Yup, that's him. I recognized him from my searches, and, well, here he is again."

The next photo was of Spree, behind a little girl he had on her knees in a bed, the girl's face looking up at the camera. It was one of the dead-eyed girls, one of the ones who showed no emotion, and she couldn't have been more than twelve. She was completely naked, staring up at the camera, with Spree behind her, also naked, holding on to one of her pig tails with his left hand, while again saluting the camera with a bottle of Heineken in his right hand, and a broad smile across his face.

"Fuck me," Tommy said in a low and sullen voice.

Roya then scrolled through a dozen or more photos, each showing Spree and the other man with different girls, performing different sexual acts on them, smiling for the camera, even when the girls were crying out in pain.

"Enough, enough, Roya. I don't want to see anymore."

"There are hundreds of them," Roya said, "And they don't get any better."

She put down her tablet on the table and they embraced. Tommy held her as tight as he would his own daughter, Caitlin. "I'm so sorry, Roya," he said softly into her ear.

Roya squeezed Tommy with every bit of strength she had, somehow trying to squeeze all the pain out of all the little girls she had just witnessed being abused.

"It's okay, Tommy, it's okay. We caught him… and now, now, they're going to pay."

They held each other tightly like that for at least another minute, before they could release and look at one another again. Roya looked up at Tommy and saw a single tear run down his cheek. In him, she saw the older brother and the father she never had, also the kind of man, she hoped one day she could find for herself.

"My god, Tommy, how do you cops even function being around this shit, fucking child rapists, murderers, liars, thieves? How can you even stand the rest of the world? How can you see this shit every day, and cope. How do you cope?" she asked.

"Somebody's got to do it, Roya…" Tommy paused, and looked her in the eye, and then down to the table,

"Somebody's got to do it," he repeated, and then he gave her a sad smile and took a drink from his bottle of Budweiser.

They sat silently for a moment, both looking at the table, then at one another, it was like they were the only two people in the place and for that moment, they were. Tommy and Roya now shared something that no one in the world, outside of Derek Spree and his victims knew of. And Roya, now, understood the bond that cops have to one another. She saw behind the veil, into their private club. She saw the extreme weight that many men and women carry with them every day, for the rest of their lives, because of the thankless job they chose.

Roya took a deep breath and lifted her glance from the table. She looked around the pub; she saw people smiling and having fun, heard them laughing, and a look came over her face as if to say, 'How dare you? How dare you all?' In her look there was anger, and in her heart, contempt; anger that people like Derek Spree existed, and contempt at all the laughing, all the happy faces at the bar... 'How dare they smile and how dare they laugh?'

Roya then looked back at Tommy. She watched him take another drink from his bottle of beer as he stared out the window onto York Avenue. She had always loved Tommy. Sure, she had a childhood crush on him when she was younger, but her love wasn't that of a lover. It was that of a young girl, seeing something special in an older, wiser person. And tonight, that love grew stronger, for now she somehow saw him as weaker, weaker than she had once thought. Weaker, in that, she saw him as a human, and not the strong and handsome superhero, she had seen so many times come home in uniform with medals rising high above the badge on his chest. No, she saw him differently. She saw him, now, more as he was -- a middle aged, divorced man, with probably a hundred or more ghosts from his past, constantly flying around inside his head.

'How do you do it?' she asked again, but this time to herself in her head. 'Somebody's got to,' she replied, then leaned over and kissed Tommy on the temple.

He turned and smiled at her. It was a sincere smile.

"Would you like another drink, Roya? I could use another beer."

"Uh, yes, absolutely, Detective." Roya stood and moved over to her original seat, sitting opposite Tommy.

Tommy returned with their drinks and sat back down, "Okay, no more Spree talk. That's not how we do it. From now on it's just social, nonsense talk," Tommy said.

"Social nonsense talk?" Roya asked.

"Yeah, social nonsense talk. You know… sports, sex, movies and music. Meaningless, stupid, nonsense talk… Nothing deep, nothing depressing. But, I'm not a sports fan, and I'm not talking sex with you either. That would just be weird."

"Okay, I agree, but I do have a sex question for you?"

"No, Roya. I said that would be weird."

"Well, I'm going to ask it anyway. Don't look, but who is that redhead at the end of the bar? She's small, so you might not see her, but she keeps looking over here."

"How am I supposed to tell you, if I can't look?" Tommy asked with a slight smile.

"Well, look… but don't make it look like you're looking," Roya smiled, shaking her head at Tommy.

Tommy casually made a glance over and saw Molly at the far end of the bar. She was the only one with reddish hair, and the only one who looked in their direction.

"I think you're asking about Molly. She works here, why do you ask?"

"You two ever do it? Is there something between you?"

"Ha ha, no, nothing at all. What makes you ask that?"

"Well, she keeps looking over here, and every time she does, she's throwing daggers with her eyes. Me thinks she likes you, and maybe is a little jealous that we're sitting together. Probably thinks we're on a date?" Roya grinned at Tommy.

"No, that's silly. Well, maybe she likes me a little, but as a good customer, and a friend. She's too young for me, Roya, and well, I'm not interested."

"You may not be interested in her, but she is definitely interested in you, Tommy," Roya replied.

"Stop now," Tommy smiled at her, "Music or movies, that's it now. I like your shirt, let's talk about them, the Airborne Toxic Event."

And so the conversation went on for a couple of hours, and Tommy and Roya talked music, and movies. They reminisced about growing up on the same block, discussed world events, and simply enjoyed one another's company, the way two comrades in arms do after a costly battle is over.

Once they both felt they had enough to drink, and felt the hour getting late, they made their way to the door, said thank you and goodnight to Jack behind the bar, and together they walked, arm in arm, back to their building on East 88th Street.

Chapter Ten

It was the Wednesday before Thanksgiving, and it also happened to be B Squad's first, of two, RDO's (Regular Days Off). Cookie had asked Tommy if he could come up to the house in Brewster, to help bring some furniture up from the basement, for the following day's dinner party.

The plan was to set up for Thanksgiving during the day, and wait for Caitlin to come home from Sienna with her new boyfriend, Nick. He would be driving the two of them down, joining Caitlin and her parents for dinner that night, before heading on out to Long Island, to be with his family for the weekend.

It had become customary over the last ten years since Cookie and Tommy had been divorced, to still spend Thanksgiving and Christmas Eve together, with Caitlin, with the few exceptions when Tommy was stuck with duty for the holidays.

On this sunny and mild Thanksgiving Eve, Tommy, who was always punctual, arrived at his wife's and daughter's house in Brewster, at 1 PM sharp. He parked in the driveway, walked up the porch steps, and rang the bell. A few seconds went by, and then he rang the bell a second time. After no answer he rang it a third. The door opened and Cookie, wearing a thin robe with Japanese print, her hair tied up in a navy scrunchie, looked Tommy in the eye.

"What the fuck you ringing the bell for, Tommy? I got stuff on the stove I'm doing for tomorrow. You can't open the fucking door yourself? How many times you been here now? You gotta interrupt me while I'm busy, rather than just walk in? ...Why you being so formal?"

"Sorry, Cook, I didn't want to walk in unannounced," he replied.

Cookie leaned out the door and kissed him on the cheek.

"Unannounced," she repeated, "What? Are you afraid you're gonna catch me in my undies? Come on in, silly, are you hungry? Did you eat yet? Can I--"

"No, no, Cookie, I'm good. I had something before I got in the car... What do you want me to do? Bring up the round oak table and chairs from the basement?"

"Yes, please. And set them up by the side of the dining room table, like we did last year, please."

"Okay, cool. How many people for dinner this year, Cookie?"

"Should be 14, if everyone shows. I wish you could get your mother up here for one of these holidays. What is she doing tomorrow? Let me guess -- she's going to go out with Sophie for an early dinner and commiserate about how nobody wants them around anymore now that they're old?"

"Yup, you got it. She and Aunt Sophie are going to head down to the old Finnegan's Wake Pub, for a typical widows' Thanksgiving. And who's not gonna show here tomorrow?"

"You know, you never know -- with that bitch sister in-law of mine -- what emergency, or invented illness, is gonna befall her."

"Ha! That woman is a trip, but they'll make it, no way Tony's gonna miss one of your dinners. And you know, your mother would never forgive him if they cancelled anyway, not last minute like that, and certainly not on Thanksgiving."

"Yeah, I know... How are you, Tommy? You have that faraway look that tells me it was a bad week at work, what's bothering you?"

Tommy was never one to talk about the job, but since their divorce he would occasionally share things with Cookie, if and when she asked. So he filled her in on the Hayden Jon Marshall case. He didn't get into details, or tell her anything about Derek Spree or what Roya had discovered, but did give her the basics of what was going on and how this little boy had now been missing for five days. Cookie listened intently. Then she moved closer to him, placed her hand on his cheek and kissed him softly, in an attempt to comfort him and let him know she understood. She then changed the subject to Caitlin, and how well she was doing at school. They chatted for about an hour over how proud they both were of her, and how well she had turned out.

Cookie, as she had learned to do over the years, had managed to deflect the conversation, and bring a slight bit of normalcy back into Tommy's life for that moment.

"Listen, I turned the stove off... I'm gonna head upstairs for a minute. When you're done with the table, there's a box with some red tape on it, by the hot water heater, it says "dining stuff" on it. Can you grab that and bring it up too, please?"

"Sure, Cook," Tommy replied.

Tommy arranged the table and chairs, where they had been set for the last few years, and dropped the box on top of the table. He then opened a bottle of water he took from the refrigerator and took a sip.

"Tommy... Tommy?"

Tommy heard Cookie yelling from upstairs.

"Yeah? What's up?" he replied, also yelling loudly, from the kitchen.

"Tommy, can you come up here, please? I need your help with something," Cookie yelled back at him.

"Yeah, I'm coming," he yelled back.

Tommy got to the top of the stairs, made the right hand turn into Cookie's bedroom, and then stopped short.

Cookie stood in front of him, leaning against the door jamb of her walk-in closet, completely naked, with the exception of a pair of black velvet, four-inch pumps with an inch and a quarter platform on them, which made her legs appear impossibly long. Her hips thrust out, and her chin tilted down low, almost onto her chest, so her large brown eyes peered innocently, straight into Tommy's. She had let her hair down and brushed it out, so it fell softly on her shoulders, and had tightened up her bangs, to give her that perfect Bettie Page look, that she knew Tommy was a complete sucker for.

Tommy stood there staring, for a good three or four seconds, when in a soft voice Cookie stated, "What are you waiting for? Get out of those jeans, Tommy."

Tommy wasted no time kicking off his shoes and pulling off his socks. His jeans quickly fell to the floor, hitting the oak with a thud, from the weight of his revolver and his wallet. He removed his underwear and was immediately erect. His shirt, and under-shirt came off quickly, as he crossed the room towards Cookie, who didn't move a muscle, other than to broaden her smile, as he approached.

Tommy first kissed Cookie softly, gently. Then again with slightly more pressure, then again even harder, as they both began to dart their tongues in and out of one another's mouths. Cookie took a deep breath, almost a small gasp, and straightened herself up onto her toes spreading her legs slightly as her passion rose. Tommy moved his mouth to her neck, kissing her, as he slowly lowered himself down her sternum and to her left breast, sucking her erect nipple into his mouth. He then slowly moved over to the right, pinching that nipple between his lips, and then sucking the entire nipple into his mouth, as Cookie's breath became more and more rapid and their body temperatures began to rise.

Tommy continued to lower himself down Cookie's body, firmly holding her by her waist with his hands as his tongue traced its way down her flat stomach and into and around her navel before then moving down between her legs, where at first he just used the tip of his tongue to flick and tease but soon found a rhythm that matched that of Cookie's now pounding heart. Within about ninety seconds or so

Cookie's body became rigid as every muscle flexed and then began to tremble in orgasm.

Tommy began to stand and as he rose his hands moved from Cookie's waist to her rear, where he cupped both of her ass cheeks, one in each hand, and lifted her from the floor, her left shoe falling from her foot. He turned and dropped her onto her bed, simultaneously climbing on top of her and slipping himself into her in one decisive and deliberate stroke. Cookie let out a short gasp, followed by an, "Oh yes."

Together they were bonded in that position as Tommy methodically thrust himself into Cookie with a steady rhythm until his body also tightened in ecstasy, followed by a long and hard exhale.

They laid intertwined, him still on top of her, for a few minutes. Then he slowly rolled off of her.

"That was great," Tommy said softly, "What made you decide to jump me this time?"

"Nothing special. I just needed it," Cookie replied "And we, we were always good this way, Tommy," she added.

They lay silently for another couple minutes, her hand resting on top of his. Then Cookie got up and headed for the bathroom door.

"I still love you, Cookie," Tommy said flatly, while staring up at the ceiling.

"I know you do, Tommy... I know you do," she repeated as she closed the door behind her.

***

Tommy got up and collected his clothes. He stepped out of the room and across the hall to his daughter's bathroom, where he washed up and got dressed. He then went downstairs and sat in front of the television in the living room, surfing through the channels but unable to find anything of interest, or anything that could shake the loneliness and desire he now felt for his ex-wife. It was a rare occasion that Tommy and Cookie got together in this way, and probably because of pride. Although Tommy still loved her deeply, intimacy was always Cookie's decision, and on Cookie's terms. Tommy had never asked for sex nor ever even kissed Cookie on the mouth since their divorce. The only exception to this rule was when Cookie made it apparent she needed him in that way. And whenever Cookie needed something, Tommy was there for her.

The only thing Cookie had never asked for in their ten years of divorce, and would never ask for, was money. And that was her pride. She had no problem having Tommy come up to move furniture, fix an appliance, service her car, or service her personally. But never would she ask Tommy for money. When they divorced there was no alimony or child support ever discussed, although her lawyer had suggested it several times.

Cookie was a woman of honor. She was the one who needed out of the marriage. She knew, and accepted, that it was she who had ended the marriage. Yes, being married to a cop, especially a cop like Tommy Keane, was hard, incredibly hard, but she couldn't blame Tommy for the fear that enveloped her each night he kissed her and left for work, wondering if it would be the last kiss, waiting for another call from one of his superiors saying he was in the hospital again, or maybe worse. And she couldn't blame Tommy for obsessing over victims and catching the criminals who terrorized the Bronx. In fact, it was his intensity that drew her to him in the first place. In Cookie's mind, Tommy was a cowboy in a white hat, a knight riding in on a white steed. He was the last of the Mohicans, and in her mind Tommy was everything a real man should be. Cookie knew she had ended the marriage for her own sanity and she never blamed Tommy for it not working out, not ever, not once. She knew Tommy was an honorable man as well, maybe honorable to a fault.

Help with raising Caitlin was never a question. Money for college or anything she needed, was never a question. And Tommy never asked Cookie where any money went, or why it was needed, when it came to his paternal responsibilities. If Caitlin needed something it was taken care of, and both Tommy and Cookie had a mutual respect for one another that was unmatched. When it came to honesty and trust in one another and in the team they formed to take care of their only child, their commitment to this estranged family unit was still as strong as the day they took their vows.

Tommy heard the click clack of Cookie's heels coming down the stairs. As she entered the room he thought, 'God damn, you are a beautiful woman,' but he said, "You look cute, Cook," then put his eyes back to the nothing he was watching on television.

"Thanks," was her one word reply as she passed him heading back into the kitchen.

"What time is Caitlin coming?" he asked as she made her way by.

"She should be here in the next 30 or 40 minutes, I think."

"And where we eating?"

"We're going to go to Town Square Pizza in Patterson. It's nice, you'll like it. I figured with all the traditional Thanksgiving stuff we're having tomorrow, some Italian would be nice tonight."

"Sounds good to me, Cookie. Good place? You like it?"

"Definitely. It's simple but you'll love it, I promise."

The time passed and Tommy started to feel at home, relaxed, and in the holiday spirit. He heard the door open and Cookie stepped from the kitchen into the living room.

"They're heeeere!" she exclaimed in a loud and drawn out manner.

Tommy stood and turned around to face the entryway, as Cookie rushed past him letting out a light squeal of happiness and excitement, as she threw her arms around Caitlin.

"Oh… Welcome home, baby! I missed you sooo much," she said placing both her hands on Caitlin's cheeks, mushing them together and giving her a large smacking kiss on the lips. "And who is this handsome young man? Is this the Nick you've been telling me about?"

"Yes, Mom, this is Nick," Caitlin replied.

Nick reached out his hand, "Nice to meet you, Mrs. Keane."

"Nonsense." Cookie said and threw her arms around Nick giving him a big kiss on the cheek along with a hearty and welcoming hug, while Caitlin rushed to her father and hugged him as hard as she could.

"I miss you so much, Daddy," she said into his chest. He hugged her back and then pulled slightly back so he could see her.

"I miss you too, sweet girl," Tommy replied, looking her in the eyes then kissing her on the forehead.

"This is Nick," she said awkwardly, motioning to the tall, handsome boy standing in the entryway.

Tommy reached out his hand and shook Nick's firmly. "Don't worry I'm not gonna kiss you just yet, Nick," Tommy said with a grin.

"Thank you, Mr. Keane, I don't know if I'm quite ready for that... but it's very nice to meet you, sir," Nick replied, also in an awkward manner. "Caitlin never stops talking about you... you both," he replied nervously, unsure about not including Cookie in his initial statement.

"Okay, let's get your bags and stuff in the house and we'll go and get something to eat. You kids hungry?" Cookie asked.

"I'm starving!" Caitlin exclaimed, "And this guy is always hungry," she said bumping her shoulder into Nick. "We're going to Town Square?" she asked.

"That's the plan," Cookie replied.

"Excellent! You're gonna love it, Nick," Caitlin said.

"It will be your father's first time, as well," said Cookie.

"Really? You've never been to Town Square, Daddy?"

"No ma'am, first time for me," Tommy replied.

"I think you'll like it. I like most everything there."

The banter between the four of them continued as they unloaded Caitlin's bags from Nick's car and brought them up the steps of the front porch.

Tommy's phone buzzed, he looked at the number and didn't recognize it. "Keane here," he answered.

"Get to Reif's now," Tommy recognized Terry's voice.

"Can it wait?" Tommy asked, knowing full well if he was getting a call from Terry there was no way the answer would be yes.

"We got a line on that woman what took the kid. Get here, now," was Terry's reply.

"I'm on my way. I should be there in less than 90 minutes."

Tommy stepped inside the entryway where the other three were gathered, smiling and making small talk. Already totally focused on what he needed to do, he walked in and gave Caitlin a huge hug, "Sorry guys, I just got a call and I have to get back to the city right away."

"Really, Daddy?" Caitlin said, as her smile disappeared from her face.

"For fuck sake, Tommy! Can't it wait?" said Cookie, staring at him in disbelief.

"It's serious, Cook. I gotta go. Sorry, Nick, it was nice meeting you," he said hugging Caitlin firmly again, "I got no time. I gotta go, I'm sorry."

He then turned and walked out of the house, got into his CRV, and started his mad dash to the city.

This was far from the first time Tommy's job or his sense of duty would get in the way of his family life. Missing holidays and family events is an occupational hazard that is basically built into the title Police Detective. Nothing is held sacred to the world of crime.

Chapter Eleven

Tommy drove like a bank robber all the way to Reif's, and on the way he called Doreen Doyle.

"Doreen, I know you're getting yourself all ready for one of the biggest bar nights of the year, but pay attention to your phone. I may be getting some info on our boy Hayden in a little more than an hour. I got no idea what, it may be nothing, but it may be everything. Just hang tight please and the second I know something, I'll let you know."

"Really! Really? Okay, Tommy, I had no big plans for tonight anyway, but I'll wait for your call. Do you want me to meet you anywhere?" she replied in an excited tone.

"No, no, not yet. I got nothing just yet, but I'll give you a call shortly either way. Okay? Just hang tight for me, kid."

"You got it, Tommy," and they hung up.

Tommy pulled onto 92nd Street, parked directly in front of Reif's and ran into the pub as quickly as he could. The moment he entered he saw Terry and his twelve year-old protégé, Shane, sitting at the far end of the bar. Terry stood and gave Tommy a head motion to follow him into the back room, and then he tapped Shane on the shoulder to alert him they were moving to the back as well.

They passed four men and a woman, who were playing pool at the pool table, then stepped out into the backyard of the pub, where two other men were smoking.

"You two, back inside, give us this space," Terry said to the two of them, who both immediately dropped their cigarettes and stepped inside.

"What do you got for me, Terry?" Tommy asked.

"Our boy Shane here saw the woman we think you're looking for, Tommy. Tell him what you saw, Shane."

"I saw her leave the black building and walk to the Gristedes market. I followed her in, watched her do her shopping and then followed her back to the building."

"You saw who, Shane? Tell me again and be specific, Shane, I need to know everything," Tommy said.

"I saw the little Spanish lady, the one with kinda Chinese eyes leave the building -- the brick buildings Terry told us to watch. She looked like the one in the picture Terry showed us, very short, kinda Puerto Rican lookin' but with Chinese eyes," he said.

"And what did she buy? Did you notice?" Tommy asked.

"Yeah, I saw her get some of those round boxes of oatmeal, you know what I mean? They're cardboard but they're round with the old pilgrim man on the front of them? And she got a couple big bags of rice and some diapers. Then she went straight back to the building. I followed her the whole way, and she never knew I was behind her."

"And what-- How did you see her? What were you--" Tommy began to ask, but was cut off.

"Terry said, Terry said for us all to hang out over there on that block and scope out that building for yous. He said if we see anyone that looks like that little woman come out or go in, to tell him right away, and if we could follow 'em, to find out where they went, and what they did. So we been hangin' out over there the last two days just you know, hangin' out, throwing the football, eatin' pizza and Chinese, waiting to see who lived there and where they went, like Terry said."

"You did great, Shane. You guys did great. Fuck yeah, you did great. Give me a minute, don't go anywhere, okay?"

Tommy pulled out his phone and put his hand on the back of Terry's head, cupping it firmly and fondly, and looked him in the eye.

"Thank you. Thank you, Terry."

He put the phone to his ear.

"Lieutenant Bricks, this is Tommy Keane. I got a line on that missing Hayden boy. Do you think, do you think you could call down to the DA's office right now and tell them we need a warrant for 148 East 82nd Street? We don't have time to be fucking around here and I know it's Thanksgiving Eve and if I ask, I'm probably going to get the run around and just going to have to get you to call 'em anyway."

"What do you know, Tommy?"

"I got a CI (Confidential Informant) who ID'd the woman we've been looking for. He's seen her leave and return to that address. She's the woman from the CCTV images we have with the boy, and it's the building on 82nd Street that we had some suspicions on, after some neighbors on the block named it as a building to watch... It's a private residence owned by Herbert Abramson. We're not sure who the woman is, she hasn't been ID'd but we know she is the subject from the abduction and we have her on tape at three different locations leading her to the block. We also know she was buying diapers at the Gristedes around the corner."

"Okay, Tommy, I'll get on the phone right away. You wanna head on down to Center Street and get it sworn? Hopefully there will be an ADA and a judge waiting for you when you arrive."

"Absolutely, and I already gave Doreen a heads up that something may be happening. I'll call her again now and have her join us if all works out."

"Very good, let me know when you arrive."

"Will do, Lu. And thank you."

Tommy stuffed his phone back in his pocket, stepped up to Terry and gave him a hug, "Thanks brother, you helped me out in a big way here."

He stuck his hand out to Shane and shook it firmly.

"And thank you, Shane. You may not realize it, but you really did a good job for me, kid. Thank you very much. I owe you one. If you ever need anything, don't be shy to ask," he looked over to Terry and shook his head towards Shane, "Our man Shane here has the makings of a good detective."

"Not likely," Shane replied.

***

Tommy left Reif's, got back into his CRV and sped down to 100 Center Street, jumping on the FDR Drive at 96th Street. On the way, he received a text from Lieutenant Bricks to meet with Assistant District Attorney Marcia Gold, who would have the warrant written up by the time he arrived.

Tommy made it to the court house without incident, and lucked out with an actual parking spot directly across the street. He ran into the building and found ADA Gold in her office with the Warrant Application written and ready.

Together ADA Gold and Tommy went to Judge Michael Rizeman's court, and were directed to his chambers. There, the Honorable Judge Rizeman, surprisingly asked nothing about the case, other than for Tommy to confirm that he did indeed have a Confidential Informant who put the alleged child abductor leaving and entering the building, which was a private residence, to which Tommy did affirm and swear to. The Judge then gave Tommy a "No-Knock" warrant authorizing the police department to enter 148 East 82nd Street the next day, which happened to be Thanksgiving Day, between the hours of 09:00 and 18:00.

Tommy thanked the Judge, stood, and shook his hand over the desk. He then turned and thanked ADA Gold for her help. She grasped his hand firmly with both of her hands and, with a bit of a panicked look, said, "Good luck, Detective. God I hope you find that boy… and God, dear God, let him be okay."

Tommy held her hand for a moment. He nodded to her, never breaking eye contact, pursed his lips tightly for a second, while the gravity of the situation took hold, and then simply replied, "Thank you, dear."

Tommy left the Judge's chambers, and as he rode the elevator down, he called Lieutenant Bricks.

"I got the warrant, Lu," Tommy said as soon as the phone was answered.

"Good man, Tom, all go smooth?"

"Yes, sir. ADA Gold had it all written out when I arrived, and Judge Rizeman didn't ask a single question. He just signed off on it and said good luck... It's dated for tomorrow morning though, 9:00 AM."

"Okay, what can I do to help, Tom?" Lieutenant Bricks asked.

"If you don't mind, Lu, can you put in a call to Emergency Services? See if we can get Truck Two or the A-Team over to the station house by like seven tomorrow morning, so we can go over everything and hit the door at nine on the dot. Maybe notify the duty captain for me as well? I'm almost in the car, heading up to the house for a bit, and like to get that confirmed and in motion."

"You got it, pal. Let me get on that now. I'll come in tomorrow morning to help you out with this one as well. And Tom, good job. I'm really glad you didn't send this one down to Missing Persons."

"Thanks, Lu."

***

It was almost 9:00 PM. Suddenly the day came to a halt.

'Is that it?' Tommy thought 'Are we set? Another few hours to go and we'll be in that house on 82nd Street. Will our boy Hayden be there? God let him be there, let him be there.'

Hayden Jon Marshall

Chapter Twelve

The Emergency Service A Team (Apprehension Tactical Team) Truck arrived at the 2-1 at 7:18 AM, and Tommy held a briefing in the muster room. Together he, along with ESU, Lieutenant Bricks, Doreen Doyle, Detective Keogh, and Detective Volpe from Squad A, Sgt. Hoya, and Officers Hernandez, Smith, and Burke, from Patrol, were all present. Tommy laid out the details of the warrant they were going to serve at 9:00 at 148 East 82nd Street, that Thanksgiving morning.

During this briefing, he gave what little information he had on the building itself, and who would be doing what, when the warrant was served.

The ESU A-Team was the official warrant truck, and the teams that were assigned to this truck were true professionals who took down doors and served warrants all over the city, all day, every day. That, as usual, was their mission today. Tommy would ride in the front of the ESU truck, which was a large, armored box truck. Upon arrival he would run up to the building and identify the door he wanted entry to, then step aside.

The ESU team of six men would then take the door by force with a large heavy iron battering ram, and, dressed in bulletproof armor with helmets, shields, and automatic weapons, do a room-by-room sweep of the entire building. They would cuff anyone they came in contact with, and then give the "All Clear" once they had secured the premises and it was deemed safe for the investigatory team (Tommy, Lieutenant Bricks, Doreen, and Detectives Keogh and Volpe, who were on duty that day for squad A) to enter. The patrol Sergeant and patrol officers were to block off the street and stop any civilians from approaching the building from either side during the execution of the warrant.

***

The ESU A-Team truck led the way. Doreen followed, with Lieutenant Bricks, Keogh and Volpe behind her, and the patrol Sergeant and officers behind them. With their lights on but sirens off, the convoy made its way up Park Avenue in next to no traffic, and then turned at 82nd Street. At this point, Tommy's heart began to beat faster. He had been on over a hundred warrants over the years, but the excitement of coming up on a building and taking the doors never got old to him. There was nothing routine about serving a no-knock warrant. It was always an exciting rush, especially when he was in Narcotics, and more often than not, he was the one swinging the ram into the door.

9:04 AM

The A-Team truck pulled up just west of 148 East 82nd Street. Tommy leapt from the truck, ran over to the stoop of the building, and pointed at the front door.

The ESU Team came up swiftly behind him, made their way up the couple of front steps, and BOOM! BOOM! BOOM! The quiet of that early Thanksgiving morning was shattered by the sound of the team's ram smashing through the front door, and the subsequent shouts of "Police! Police! Get Down! Police! Get Down on the floor now! Get Down! Get Down!"

It was probably less than two, possibly three minutes, but waiting outside for the "All Clear" felt like an eternity to Tommy, who was so anxious to gain entry and hopefully, hopefully find Hayden alive and well.

"All Clear!" came from inside, and an ESU Officer repeated it out the front door. Tommy, followed by Doreen, Lieutenant Bricks, Keogh, and Volpe, all entered the house.

"Up here, Detectives! Up here," they could hear one of the ESU officers yelling. Tommy quickly headed up the first flight of stairs as he continued to hear from above, "Up here, on the third floor."

As he made it up the second flight of stairs, he could see the very small Filipino woman lying face down in the prone position with her hands cuffed behind her back, a 200-plus pound ESU Officer over her with a Mini-14 rifle pointed in her direction.

"In here, Detective, in here," another ESU Officer, who stood in the doorway to a room at the top of the stairs, waved at Tommy to come in. "I think you found what you were looking for, Detective, plus a little more. I'd say you hit the jackpot here, pal," The ESU Officer continued to say, speaking so loudly in the excitement, he was almost shouting.

"What the fuck?" Tommy said out loud when he reached the doorway, and froze in disbelief for a second. There he was... Tommy was looking at little Hayden Jon Marshall.

He was alive, alive and well, and cowering in the far corner of the room. He was dressed in a white t-shirt, white briefs, and white socks. Hayden was alive and in the company of several other boys and girls. The children appeared to be between the ages of three and maybe fourteen years of age, and each one of them was dressed exactly the same way: in very clean, pure white cotton t-shirts, briefs, and socks. Together they huddled tightly in the far corner. Some of them were hugging and holding onto one another out of fear of the large helmeted police officers who had just smashed and crashed into the room they were being held in. Some physically shook in fear. Some cried out-loud, at least one urinated on himself, but they all packed themselves into the corner of that room together, just as tightly as they could, to avoid the noise, and the ominous presence of the men who had just come to liberate them.

Tommy stepped into the room and Doreen, who was right behind him, stopped in the doorway. He got down on one knee, looked at Hayden, and in a very soft and paternal voice, spoke out to him. "Hayden? Hayden, it's okay buddy, it's okay. I'm a friend of your mommy and daddy's. I'm a police man, Hayden, it's okay."

Hayden was visibly shaken and he stood very still, crying and shaking his head no.

"C'mon, buddy… It's okay. My name is Tommy, and I'm friends with your mommy, Jessica, and your daddy, David. I know you, Hayden. It's okay little buddy, we are friends… Can you… Can you come to me, little buddy? C'mon, c'mon over here, and I'll take you home to your mommy, Jessica, she misses you very much. Would you like to go home and see mommy?"

As he continued with his coaxing, little Hayden let loose of the other children and rushed the five or six steps into Tommy's arms. Tommy hugged him tight and stood up with Hayden in his arms and Hayden's arms wrapped around his neck.

Holding him tightly, Tommy then looked at the other children in the corner, and in his same soft, paternal voice, asked the room in general, "And who are all your friends here, Hayden?"

Hayden Jon Marshall

Chapter Thirteen

When the A-Team entered the building, the focus was on its inhabitants, finding Hayden, and securing the building for all involved. That meant any possible threat had to be neutralized, and therefore all focus was placed on any persons who were found in the premises.

Upon entry, the entire home was searched methodically, room by room, from the first floor to the third, and down into the basement. Each floor was found to be empty and cleared but for the third, where one female was found and detained on the third floor landing, and one elderly male was found and detained in the front room, which faced the street.

Eight children, aged three to approximately fourteen, had been found and held in the back room of that third floor. During the serving of the warrant, nothing else was immediately noted by the entry team, or even by the detectives, until all had been secured and everyone was able to take a breath for a moment. And then, one by one, just about every ESU Officer and every detective on scene began to utter, almost collectively… "What the fuck?" and for some of them the sentiment was repeated several times.

Almost everything within the confines of the home was painted a gloss white. The ceilings, the walls, the floors, every piece of furniture, absolutely everything was painted gloss white. All of the appliances in the kitchen were white, as were the pure white Corian countertops, white tile floors in the kitchen as well as in the bathrooms. Anything that wasn't 100% white was chrome, and the place was completely immaculate. The only thing that wasn't white was the red construction/building paper that lined the hallway floors and the detectives assumed that paper was taped to the floor to keep it clean from the white socked feet of all the home's inhabitants.

Every child found in the back upstairs bedroom wore a new, clean white t-shirt, white socks, and white boy briefs, even the girls. The woman, who lay on the floor of the third story hallway, also wore the same, although she had a pure white terry cloth bathrobe on over her tighty-whitey ensemble. The elderly man, who was found in the front room of the third floor, also wore a clean, new white t-shirt, white briefs, and white socks, and in his case he also had on a pure white terry cloth bathrobe.

The room the children were in was the largest, and had nothing in it but bunk beds -- four custom-built, three-level bunk beds, making the room resemble a bunk room in a submarine. There was enough room to accommodate twelve people. The beds were all painted in the same gloss white paint, and all the sheets and blankets were also pure white.

In the hallway, next to the bunk room where the children slept, was a bathroom with two toilets and two sinks. Next to that room was another bathroom, which was nothing more than a large shower room: a large, custom tiled area, with three shower heads, so three people could shower at a time. The next room was very small, but served as a utility closet, with shelves packed with cleaning supplies and paper products.

The next room, at the end of the hall, had a sign on the door that simply read 'HQ Please Knock.' This was obviously considered the headquarters room. It was a decent sized room, but smaller than the children's room. Again, everything in it was white. This room had a large desk centered on the door, so when left open, whoever was seated in it could look straight down the hall to the room that housed the children. There were built-in bookshelves, and custom wooden filing cabinets that lined the walls. Every book on the shelves was wrapped in a white paper book cover, with its content written on the spine. On the desk sat two monitors. One was a computer monitor, connected to the internet, and the other was a security monitor, which was connected to sixteen cameras throughout the interior and exterior of the house.

On the second floor there were two bedrooms. The one in the front of the building, directly below the HQ room, was tastefully appointed, although again, absolutely everything was pure white. Attached to the bedroom was a large master bath, done completely in white, and attached to both the bedroom and master bath, was a large walk-in closet. Inside the closet there were white, cubby-holed shelves containing dozens of neatly folded white t-shirts and briefs, and neatly rolled white cotton socks. On rods, hung about ten white terry cloth bathrobes, and five thin white linen robes. Tucked to one side of the rod, amazingly, were three black Brooks Brothers suits with matching black ties, white Brooks Brothers dress shirts, and three pairs of matching, very clean and highly polished, black leather Oxfords, along with two identical black Brooks Brothers woolen overcoats.

On the opposite side of the second floor, was a mirror image of the front bedroom. Again everything was white, with an almost identical bathroom and walk-in closet. The contents inside the closet were also almost identical, with the cubby holes and white clothing. However, hanging on the rods were several different sets of clothing and other accessories, all to fit a woman of a smaller stature. Included on this rack of clothing was a long black down coat, which was reversible, and was white on the inside.

On the first floor was a large room that was configured almost like a classroom. There were large white boards on the walls, along with many, many, nicely framed, very large photos of the universe and different solar systems. There were some boxes of toys and some simple games, including checkers, chess, Connect Four, and other fairly innocuous games. All of the boxes were wrapped in white paper with the name of the contents written on the outside.

The next room was a small bathroom with two toilets and two sinks, and then a large eat-in kitchen that housed a narrow, twelve-foot long dining table surrounded by chairs, again all in white.

And if all of this white, chrome, and stainless steel wasn't strange enough, it appeared that every food item in the house was white as well. The cabinets were stocked full with white rice, barley, pasta, oatmeal, and cannellini beans. The refrigerator had a few gallons of fat free milk and seltzer water, the freezer had pounds of cod fish fillets, chicken breasts, and low carb vanilla ice cream.

Every window in the house had nice, old fashioned, wood shutters on the interior, all of which were screwed and painted shut. The shutters in the HQ room were the only ones with working louvers, but even when they were fully opened, one could only see outside through the narrow 3/8 inch gaps between the slats.

With everyone in the house dressed in nothing but white cotton underwear, the entire home was kept at a constant 75 degrees, a temperature that was now beginning to make the detectives, and even more so the ESU officers, slightly uncomfortable.

Hayden Jon Marshall

Chapter Fourteen

Tommy's head began to spin for a moment. He had been on hundreds of warrants; he had been in, and seen, unbelievably bad crime scenes that no one should ever see. He had seen adults and children living in squalor and such filthy conditions that no human should live in, and when he entered this home, this very attractive and exceptionally expensive home on Manhattan's Upper East Side, he was completely prepared for the worst. He knew full well that there could be a dead child, or a brutalized and sexually molested child in the home, if there was a child at all.

But this scene was so surreal, so Twilight Zone, so Black Mirror, that it couldn't be real. Was he dreaming this? No, he was living it. He was standing in an immaculately clean, white house, on top of red building paper, next to heavily armed ESU Officers, holding a three year-old boy he had been searching for, for the last six days.

It took a minute to digest, but yes, this scene was real. He stepped toward the door, and spoke softly to Hayden, "Hey Hayden, this is my friend, Doreen. She's really good friends with your mommy, Jessica. Can she hold you for a minute?"

Hayden, who had now stopped crying, nodded yes, in that hard up and down that toddlers do.

"Hey, Dee, can you hold this little guy for a minute, and keep an eye on these little ones in here, while I see what else we have going on here?"

"Yeah, of course," she replied, taking Hayden in her arms, "Hey, Hayden, how you doing?" she said to the child.

Tommy stepped over the silent body of the woman on the floor, and made his way to the front room of the house.

In this room, also face down in the prone position and with his hands cuffed behind his back, was the 70 year-old Herbert Abramson -- the reclusive, multi-millionaire, Wall Street wiz kid of the 1980's, who had vanished from public life almost thirty years ago.

He was short, about 5'6", and thin. He had pure white hair that was receding deeply, but not so much to leave him bald on top, and white framed glasses that sat crooked on his face after being forced to the floor and cuffed by the ESU Officer.

Tommy walked in the room and stood over the body, "Mr. Abramson, I presume?" he said intentionally with a bit of his signature sarcasm.

"You don't know what you are doing, Officer," Mr. Abramson stated in a low, rather agitated, manner.

"Listen, I'm going to help lift you up and spin you around so you are sitting on your ass. I think you'll be more comfortable that way. Please help me out and don't make this difficult, okay? Then I'm going to ask you a few questions, Mr. Abramson... Okay? Do you understand me, Mr. Abramson?"

"I understand everything. I understand more than you will ever know. The question is, do you understand? Do you understand? That is the question."

"Okay, Mr. Abramson, here we go." Tommy lifted the man up and spun him around, so he was now sitting upright on the floor, in the middle of the room marked HQ. Tommy bent over at the waist and gently straightened Mr. Abramson's glasses so they sat properly on his face.

The old man was obviously shaken, and it took a moment for him to balance himself properly, even though he was sitting securely on the floor. His exposed knees were both a bright red from where they had hit the white hardwood floors. Tommy straightened him up a bit, closing his robe and adjusting his shoulders so the old man could lean back against the desk.

"Okay, Mr. Abramson, are you a little more comfortable now?"

"No... No, I am not comfortable at all," he said, still in a monotone voice, staring straight ahead and not making eye contact with anyone in the room. "I am not comfortable with this. What gives you the right? What gives you the right?"

"The right, sir? The right? The City of New York, sir, has given me the right to come here in search of," Tommy had to stop for a second, "In search of these children." Tommy realized he had stumbled across a much deeper mystery, and a larger crime, or sets of crimes, than just the kidnapping of little Hayden.

"The Disciples you speak of are the chosen ones, and you have no right, Officer. You have no right."

"No, sir, I have every right. I need you to tell me who all of these children are and when you abducted... took... got them?"

"Those are the Disciples, you fool. You don't understand and will never understand the importance of what we do here, and the mischief you are about to unleash on the universe today."

"Listen to me now, Mr. Abramson. I need some information from you. Please sir, can you tell me who these children are and who they belong to?"

"They are the Disciples," he said indignantly. "These are eight of the twelve I am to acquire. They will rule the heavens for eternity. Once you are all dust, they will shine upon the dead and dusty earth for millennia."

"Listen, Mr. Abramson, are you going to help me out here, or are you a complete looney toon? I need to know who these children are. Please stop the nonsense talk and tell me who these children are."

"They are the eight of the twelve, you fool--"

"The twelve? Are there more children here?"

"There will be. And once we have the full circle of Disciples, they will rule the heavens for eternity, you fool. For eternity! You and your kind will never understand."

Tommy stood up straight, "Okay, I'm done with this guy for right now." He left the room and made his way over to the woman in the hallway. As he did, the ESU Sergeant was just arriving at the top of the stairs.

"You're all clear here, Detective, top to bottom, basement to roof. Anything else we can do for you? If not, we're gonna move out."

"I think we are good, my friend."

"Okay, very good, and hey Keane... Great job here."

"Thanks, pal," Tommy replied.

Tommy then leaned down and lifted the little woman off the floor and sat her back down against the wall. He could see Mr. Abramson looking down the hall at the two of them.

"Hey, Keogh, do me a favor, will you? And step inside there with Mr. Abramson and close the door while I talk to our little friend here."

"Sure thing, Tom," Keogh replied.

"And how you makin' out in there, Doreen? All cool?" Tommy asked.

"We're okay, Tommy," Doreen replied.

Tommy looked in and saw her sitting on the floor with Hayden in her lap. Four of the other children were now sitting around her, and three were still in the corner. Softly he asked, "I'm going to close this door for a minute, okay?"

"Sure, Tommy, we're okay in here."

Tommy closed the door and went back to the woman on the floor.

"Alright, so how about you? Are you going to help me out? And maybe help yourself out?"

The woman turned her face away from Tommy.

"Listen. Listen, we know it was you who snatched that little boy in there out of the park. We know everything about it." She refused to look at him.

"We have you catching the cab on 125th Street, then stealing the boy in the park from his mother, then getting on the train on 96th Street, then getting off the train at 86th, and walking right back here to this house with him. We got it all, little sister, we got it all. And that's a life sentence. Kidnapping is a life sentence, did you know that? And once we connect the dots with these other children, I bet you and old man Abramson in there will be doing quite a bit more than one life sentence, unless you help me now. You hear me? You need to help me right now, lady."

She refused to speak, and when Tommy stepped around her, to face her again, she just turned her head away again.

Tommy looked over to Detective Volpe and Lieutenant Bricks, who were still standing on the steps. "How's the place looking, Lu?"

"Place is empty, everyone in the building is right here. Obviously we got some searching to do, but really I think we are good. What you wanna do? Call for a couple busses (ambulances) for these two nuts, and CPS (Child Protective Services) for the kids? Not much we can do with them on our own here, you want me to call 'em all, while you do your interviews here?"

"Yeah, Lu, that would be great, thanks."

Tommy pushed the door open to the room where Doyle sat with the kids. He took a photo of little Hayden in

Doyle's arms with his phone, and then he called Jessica Marshall.

"Hello, Jessica? We have him, we have Hayden and he is fine, perfectly fine." Jessica Marshall screamed so loudly that Doreen could hear her exclaim, "Oh my god" over Tommy's phone from at least twelve feet away. "What's that?" Tommy continued, "No, there appears to be no harm done to him at all, I'm happy to say. No you can't come here right now, he's going to be taken to a hospital first, to make certain he's alright, but, he sure looks alright to me. Yes, ma'am, I'm going to let you know where he's going as soon as I find out, okay?... Okay let me go now, I have a lot of stuff to do, and I'm going to send you a photo of him now, that I just took... Yes, yes, thank you... I'll call you very soon, Mrs. Marshall. Okay, goodbye."

Tommy took a deep breath, then wiped a tear from his eye that was just beginning to form. 'We got him,' he said to himself in his head. Then he looked at Doreen, who was holding young Hayden, and repeated it aloud "We got him!" and Doreen smiled back, a tear running down her cheek with the realization of what they had accomplished on this Thanksgiving morning.

Tommy then stepped into the bathroom and called his newspaper contact, Gil Nunez.

"Detective Keane? Happy Thanksgiving," was the answer on the other end.

"Gil, you want a story? 148 East 82nd Street, and now. That's it, I can't talk, come now."

"Wait, what?"

"148 East 82nd Street, Gil. And if you ain't got a photographer, bring a camera. You'll be happy you came." Tommy hung up.

As Tommy stepped out of the bathroom, Lieutenant Bricks said, "Busses are on the way, and CPS notified and sending people, too."

"Thanks, Lu. Hey, Tony, keep an eye on this one, will ya?" he said pointing to the small woman sitting on the floor.

"Yup you got it, Tommy," Tony Volpe replied.

***

Tommy went back into the room with the kids, pushed the door almost all the way shut, and got down on one knee next to Doreen and Hayden.

"Hey, guys, how we doing?" All of the kids stared at him blankly, "My name is Tommy. You guys want to tell me who you are?"

None of them said a word.

"Okay, let's try this again. I'm Tommy… This is my friend, Doreen, and this guy you already know, and his name is Hayden, and he's my friend also… You, there, you look like you're the oldest," Tommy pointed to a painfully thin, ashy skinned black boy of about fourteen. "Can you tell me your name?"

No answer.

"Okay, how about you?" Tommy pointed to one of the taller girls.

Again, no answer. Then a younger girl spoke up.

"She is number two," a little girl of about ten said. She had long black hair, weaved into two plaits.

"Number two?" Tommy asked, looking over at Doreen with confusion, "Okay, and who are you, pretty girl?"

"I am number four," the little girl answered.

"Wow, you're a good talker, aren't you? Can you tell me what you used to be called? What your mom and dad called you?"

She looked at him strangely, "I'm number four," she said again, slightly confused.

"You don't remember your name? It's okay, you can tell us your name, we're all friends here."

The little girl stared at Tommy for a moment, not quite sure what he was getting at. "I'm number four," she repeated.

"Okay, can you tell me everyone else's names?" Tommy asked.

And right down the line she went, pointing at each child.

"Number one, number two, number seven, number five, number six, number three, number eight, and I am number four."

"So, my friend Hayden here, is number eight?"

"Yes. Number eight... number eight," she repeated, pointing at Hayden, then said, "Number four," putting her index finger on the top of her head.

"And I'm number five," a little blonde boy said proudly, wanting to join in.

"Alright, now we're getting somewhere… Can anyone tell me the lady's name, outside on the floor?"

Three of them nodded yes.

"Okay, how about you? We haven't heard from you yet. You're number six, right?

A little girl nodded her head and then put her thumb in her mouth.

"Okay, what is that lady's name outside in the hall there?"

"She Assa," the little girl replied.

"Assa? She doesn't look like an Assa to me, but if you say so. How about the old man, what is his name? The man with the white hair?"

"Him Asser," number four and number six said in unison.

"Okay, very good, Asser and Assa. One minute and I'll be right back, okay guys."

Tommy left the room, closing the door again behind him, and went back to the other room where Mr. Abramson was.

"Okay, Mr. Abramson, what is going on here? Or should I call you, Asser?… Huh? What's going on here, Asser?"

"You will never understand. You are a fool, a cretin, unworthy. It would take me a thousand lifetimes to explain it to you, and even then it would be beyond your grasp."

"Oh, here we go again… Listen to me!" Tommy said, now louder and more aggressively, "Who are these children?"

"They are the Disciples. They are the eight of the twelve, they are the chosen ones and they will rule the heavens for eternity."

"Okay and who is Asser?"

"Asser is the vessel; Asser is the educator, the tiller of fields, and the sower of seeds, the vessel that carries."

Tommy looked over at Keogh, whose six-foot-four, 272 pound body was sitting in the office chair, his feet up and crossed at the ankle resting on Asser the Vessel's desk.

"You getting any of this, Keogh?"

"Fuck if I know, Tommy. This whole place is fucking unreal, man, I'm just waiting for Scotty to beam this nutty fucker up."

"Unreal, that's an understatement," Tommy stood up straight and looked at Keogh, lounging with his feet up on the desk, "Comfortable, Keogh?"

"As I can get," he replied, with a sly smile.

Tommy went back to the woman sitting on the floor.

"Hey, Assa… Assa, what you got for me, anything yet?" The woman just turned her head away.

At that moment, an EMT and his partner could be heard coming up the stairs. "Hello?... Hello, is this where the EDPs (Emotionally Disturbed Persons) are? Cops outside said to come on up."

"Yeah, this way," Detective Volpe answered.

"Okay, we got two busses downstairs. You want gurneys or can they walk out?"

"Nah, we'll bring them out to yous," Volpe answered, then called out to Tommy, "Tommy, busses are here for your EDPs."

"Cool," Tommy replied, stepping back into the office. "I know you're on a break there, Keogh, but what say you help escort Mr. Abramson downstairs with me."

Tommy bent over, grabbed Mr. Abramson from behind and lifted him up onto his feet. As they stepped out of the room, Detective Volpe already had the woman up on her feet and had begun walking her down the stairs. As Tommy led the man down the stairs, Mr. Abramson continued to talk nonsense.

"You fools, you ignorant cretins! You know not what you do."

As they stepped out into the sunlight, Tommy could see there was a small crowd of maybe eight or ten people across the street. One of them was Rudy Barr, who smiled, nodded, and gave a thumbs up to Tommy when they made eye contact.

He also saw Gil Nunez running down the block from the left, and he told Keogh and Mr. Abramson to wait for one second, as they stood on the steps of the stoop, giving Gil just enough time to snap several photos with his phone.

Both Abramson, Asser, and his accomplice Assa, were loaded into the ambulances. Tommy asked Sergeant Hoya if he could send two patrol officers along with them to the hospital, because it was Thanksgiving and no one was working in the Squad. As he, Keogh, and Volpe headed back to the building, Gil Nunez approached and asked, "Detectives, excuse me, Detectives, may I ask what's going on?"

Tommy didn't have to say anything, as Keogh immediately spoke up.

"What are you, a reporter right? This is Detective Thomas Keane here. He found that little missing boy from John Jay Park. Bosses wanted to kick it down to Missing Persons, right, but Detective Keane here, he hung onto it. Now here we are on Thanksgiving morning. He not only found the kid, but he found some sorta weird ass space-age cult, and looks like we got eight or ten kids he saved here. So stick around, we'll be bringing them out soon, too. And maybe instead of bashing the cops in whatever fuckin' rag you write for, you tell the city that today, on Thanksgiving Day, they can give thanks for Detective Tommy Keane, a real fuckin' hero. Huh, how bout you right that in your paper, pal?"

"I think I will! Can I quote you on that, Detective?"

"Be my guest. And it's Keogh, K-E-O-G-H. If you're gonna use my name, spell the fuckin' thing right."

***

Back inside the building, they decided Tommy would begin searching the HQ room on the third floor, and Keogh and Volpe would begin in the basement, while Doreen stayed with the kids in the bedroom as they waited for CPS to arrive.

Tommy started in one corner of the room and began going through the bookshelves. Mr. Abramson had volumes and volumes of textbooks on the universe and space travel. So much so, that they took up half of the room. This, Tommy had little interest in. What he did find that fascinated him were as many as 200 hard-covered log books filled with Mr. Abramson's rantings, theories, and beliefs as to what was going to happen in the future, and how he, Asser, was to be the vessel for the chosen few, who would rule the heavens. Tommy pulled the books off the shelves and stacked them on the floor to take into evidence.

But Tommy had no time to get into any of that reading right then. He just needed to gather any evidence that may help the District Attorney's office prosecute the two responsible for the kidnapping of Hayden Jon Marshall and the other children.

As Tommy stacked books in the middle of the floor, Detective Volpe shouted from the bottom of the stairs,

"Tommy! Hey Tommy, come down to the basement, we got something to show you."

"Okay," Tommy replied and he started down the stairs, meeting Volpe on the first floor, where they both headed down to the basement.

The basement, like the rest of the house, was immaculate, and everything, even the floors, were painted white. Tommy, following Volpe, walked towards the back of the basement, where Detective Keogh stood over a large white trunk.

"Watcha got, Keogh?" Tommy asked.

"We got a kid's body, Tommy. It's a little girl, poor little honey, she's mummified. Take a look."

"Ahh... Fuck me." Tommy said, as he stood across the trunk from Keogh, both looking down at the mummified body of a girl, who was probably the height of a six-year-old. They both stood silently for a moment, unconsciously paying respect to the tiny body.

"Fuckin' shame," Keogh finally said softly, to break the silence.

"Okay, I'll call Crime Scene," Tommy said.

"Already did," Keogh replied.

Tommy got down on one knee and looked at the little girl. She was dressed in a pretty, white lace dress, and had a shroud of some sort of fine lace fabric placed over her body. She lay on what appeared to be two down pillows in white pillowcases. Tommy stood up, still staring at the body, and Keogh spoke out again.

"This has got to be the weirdest fuckin' day of my life, and I've had some weird fuckin' days on this job, let me tell you that."

The three detectives left the basement and waited for Crime Scene and the Medical Examiner to arrive.

***

Twenty minutes after the detectives discovered the body in the basement of the building, CPS arrived. They knew what they were coming for and arrived in two large vans with a team of five people. By this time, Doreen and Tommy had a decent rapport with the children who would speak. They collected their clothes, which only consisted of the simple cotton underwear items they wore every day. Since both Mr. Abramson and Assa were short people, the detectives were able to use their bathrobes to cover the children, and act as warmer outer garments. Together, the detectives and the CPS agents walked the children down to the first floor. Doreen carried Hayden in her arms.

Upon reaching the entranceway of the building on the first floor, something happened that none of the adults involved had expected. When Detective Volpe, who led the group, opened the front door and began to lead the children out, the eldest four or five children completely lost control of themselves. They began violently screaming and crying in fear. They thrashed about, some tried running back inside, they grabbed onto the door jambs and once outside, they grabbed onto the railings of the front stoop; they were terrified. No one understood it at first. What would make these children freak out in such a bizarre way?

It was the sun.

All of these children had been abducted at the age of two or three, and all of them had lived for years without ever seeing the sun. On this bright Thanksgiving afternoon, the sun was something none of them but the youngest were prepared for. The eldest boy, who was rather thin and frail and appeared to be about fourteen years old, was actually eighteen. But the years of malnutrition he suffered on a diet of small amounts of nothing but white foods, kept him from growing properly, and he had the worst reaction to the sun, which he hadn't seen in sixteen years, since his abduction at the age of two.

The CPS agents and the detectives eventually got all the kids into one of the vans and they were all taken to the hospital to be examined. Little Hayden, the only one of the eight that was identified, was finally back in his parent's arms at about midnight that night by the time the hospital and CPS had cleared him.

After all the children were loaded up and the vans took off, the detectives went back inside to continue their search and wait for Crime Scene and the Medical Examiner to come remove the little girl's body from the basement. Except for Tommy, who first stepped across the street to where a crowd of maybe fifteen people now stood watching what was happening. Among them was Rudy Barr, who stood with Tommy's childhood friend, Terry Callahan, and Terry's little runner, Shane.

Tommy shook Rudy's hand firmly, then Terry's, and finally Shane's.

"Thank you. If it weren't for you three we wouldn't have found these kids today… Terry, again, thanks for the introduction, and Rudy, thank you so much for pointing out the buildings, and Shane, fucking Shane, the man of the hour, thanks for staking the place out for me, brother. You did a really good thing here. You saved eight kids, man. If I can ever help you with anything, you let me know." And with that he actually saw the young, tough Shane smile, albeit for only a second.

On his way back to the building, he stopped and spoke briefly to Gil Nunez, who called out to him.

"Detective… Detective, may I have a minute, please?" Gil shouted as if he didn't know Tommy by name.

"Hey Gil, I got miles of work here to get through. If you're available, I'll text you when I'm done. If you have time, we'll meet and I'll tell you all about this whacked out story... Cool?"

"Most definitely, Detective. Please text me, no matter how late, no worries, man. You say where and when and I'll be there," Gil replied.

"Very good. It's still early now, give me five to eight hours, depending on when Crime Scene and the Medical Examiner are done, and I'll send you a text."

"The M.E.? Someone? Someone is dead?" Gil asked in a dreadful tone.

"Yes, we found the mummified remains of a child in the basement. I'll tell you about everything later when we meet."

"Okay, okay. Thank you, Detective, thank you."

***

Tommy, Doreen, Lieutenant Bricks, Keogh and Volpe spent the next six hours collecting evidence and waiting for Crime Scene and the Medical Examiner to arrive and do their investigations. The Medical Examiner, M.E. Joseph Piel, a tall, thin, balding man of about 35, said he believed the young girl found in the basement had been dead for about four years. He also said he had no way of knowing that until he did the autopsy, but by the state she was in, that was his initial guess.

By about 10:15 everything that the team could do was done, and the house was sealed with an official NYPD Crime Scene sticker. Everyone went back to the precinct, where

Tommy and Doreen vouchered what evidence they had removed from the home until about midnight or so, as Lieutenant Bricks, Keogh, and Volpe signed out for the day.

As Doreen and Tommy finished up, Tommy texted Gil Nunez. "1:00 Brady's Pub, 82nd and 2nd."

He immediately received a reply, "I'll be there."

Tommy arrived about five minutes early to find Gil waiting on a stool, in the corner of the pub, across from the bar, drinking an Absolut and Cranberry. Tommy nodded his head to Gil, asked the bartender for a Budweiser and joined Gil in the corner.

"Thank you so much for the call, Detective Keane. And thank you so much for meeting me here," Gil said as he stood and shook Tommy's hand.

"Please call me Tommy, Gil, and no problem. This is another one of those stories that needs to be told, and needs to be told right. So who else was I going to call?"

"Thank you, sir. I do so very much appreciate this, you have no idea… So this is the little boy that went missing from John Jay park last week? And it looks like you have stumbled across several other children while investigating this case, please tell me what you can."

"I'll tell you everything I know, Gil. And get ready, it's a strange one."

Tommy and Gil closed Brady's Pub that night, the bartender chasing them out at 3:45 AM. It was too late to make the morning paper, but Gil had enough information to get the front page, plus a two-page spread inside the Saturday edition, which would include several photographs.

***

Thanksgiving Day, Thursday, was now Friday, and was Tommy's first work day of the week. Lieutenant Bricks had told him to bang in for the day if he wanted, but it was a night shift, so after meeting with Gil, he headed home for a few hours' sleep, then got up, took little JoJo for a walk, chatted with his mother, and headed back into the precinct for his scheduled tour.

When he arrived, Sergeant Ruffallo and Officer Rios were behind the desk and they both stood and clapped their hands when Tommy entered the building. With that, two other officers and a PAA, stepped out of the 124 room (clerical office) and also began clapping their hands.

"Good job, Keane," Sergeant Ruffallo shouted as Tommy headed up the stairs.

As Tommy passed Charice Tate's desk, she called out, "God bless you, Detective Keane. I am so proud to know you, and so happy you saved them kids."

"Thank you, Charice," Tommy replied softly and with a smile.

Tommy entered the squad room where he found Stein sitting at his desk, "Nice job, Tommy... Nice job," was his greeting, as he finished clipping on his tie and closing his briefcase.

"Thanks, Mark, I just got lucky with this one."

"Bullshit, you worked it… You worked it like you always do, and you found that little guy and closed how many other cases? There was no luck involved at all, Tommy, that was all you and Doreen."

"Thanks, Mark, I appreciate it," Tommy replied, taking off his leather coat and sitting down at the battered desk across from Stein. "Now I gotta get back to all this other shit I got piling up though…"

Tommy was interrupted by Sergeant Browne, who walked out of his office.

"Great job on that Missing, Keane. I want to, well… I want to apologize for barking at you the other day to send it to Missing Persons. If you had… well, if you had, those children may have never been found. You did a great job with this one and I'm sorry if I made things more difficult."

"No, don't mention it," Tommy replied.

"I also have some good news for you on that Gillstone case."

"Really? What? What do you have on that?" Tommy asked.

"Well, Mr. Gillstone called me today. He wanted to speak to you. It turns out he and the family spent Thanksgiving at their home in the Hamptons, and it was there that they found Mrs. Gillstone's earrings. They were never stolen, just misplaced, or left at the other house and Mrs. Gillstone didn't know until she found them in her nightstand… Mr. Gillstone sends his sincerest apologies."

"No shit… hmm, okay. Case closed on the Gillstone's."

"I'm also sorry I gave you a hard time about that case Tommy, I had no idea."

"Of course you didn't, Sergeant Browne, how could you?" Tommy then turned his attention back to Mark Stein. "So Mark, what you got going today? You want to grab something to eat early or wait a couple hours for meal?"

Sergeant Browne waited for a moment, then turned and walked back into his office once he realized the conversation was over.

Chapter Fifteen

Over a week had passed since young Hayden and the other seven children had been found. The news was still all abuzz with the description of the children, the cult house of horrors on 82nd Street, the strange rich recluse, and the one loyal follower, who ruined so many lives.

Gil Nunez was again being hailed as a journalist extraordinaire for his scoop on the Abramson Millionaire Cult case, which now locked him in at his paper as the rising star of reporters in the city.

But for Tommy, and the rest of the 2-1 squad, it was back to work as usual. Back to the daily grind of the weekly caseload, back to Sergeant Browne and Lieutenant Bricks asking for cases to be closed, and Captain Peleggi stressing about the weekly COMPSTAT meeting down at One Police Plaza.

But on this particular day, it was beautiful and mild -- a nice late November day in New York City. It was Tommy's regular day off, or RDO as they say in the police department, and he decided he would take little JoJo for a nice long walk and enjoy the morning.

He and JoJo headed down First Avenue to Glaser's Bakery, where he picked up a cup of hot tea, a brownie, and a black and white cookie. The German bakery was a family run business that had been in Yorkville since 1902, and had invented the black and white, when they first opened over a hundred years ago. The elderly lady at the counter greeted him with a smile, "Hello, love! We haven't seen you for a while. What a darling little puppy you have there," she commented.

Tommy thanked her and then left, heading down to Carl Schurz Park, where he let JoJo run around the dog run for almost an hour. Little JoJo tormented a much larger Brindle Pit Bull and a German Short Haired Pointer, by relentlessly chasing and nipping at their legs and jowls while giving out his puny high pitched barks at the two older and much larger dogs. For the most part, the other dogs just taunted, and then ran from JoJo, until all three tired of the game.

Tommy and JoJo then sat by the river for a bit, watching a tugboat push a large barge down the East River, while looking out over Randall's Island. Tommy took what he had left of his brownie and shared it with JoJo but told him, "Chocolate is not supposed to be good for dogs there, little guy, so don't tell no one I gave this to you, okay?"

JoJo sat snug against Tommy, with his front legs up on Tommy's lap, and he too looked out onto the river watching the tugboat go by. The expression on his little pushed-in face looked more like an old man than a now sixteen-pound puppy.

Tommy didn't bother to reflect on the past week's work, or the previous week's rescue of the children on Thanksgiving Day. That case was closed, and there was nothing pressing or difficult currently sitting in his stack of open cases to worry about. This morning Tommy let his mind be free of thought, and he just enjoyed the sun with his little friend JoJo.

"Okay boy, let's head home. That's enough of the park for today."

Tommy and JoJo headed back towards the apartment, JoJo receiving comments along the way from passersby about how handsome and cute he was. Two young girls stopped them, having to take selfies with JoJo as they walked west along 87th Street. Then, when they passed a very tall man, Tommy heard from behind.

"Hey! Hey! Excuse me... I think... Hey! That's my dog!" The man said in an aggressive tone.

Tommy turned around and eyed the man, immediately sizing him up, as the automatic rolodex in his brain did with just about everyone he ever met.

The man stood about six-foot-three, with a short well-kept retro haircut. It was slicked back with some sort of heavy hair product, parted on the side with a slight pompadour in front, and a long, but equally well-kept, beard that he had pulled out from his brown and tan checked Kufiya Scarf, which was tied around his neck. He wore a dark brown corduroy sport coat over a bulky sweater and very clean, tapered blue jeans with horizontal holes in the knees that were cuffed up above his ankles, no socks, and worn, but highly polished, brown leather dress shoes.

Both Tommy and little JoJo tilted their heads to one side inquisitively as they waited for the next words to come out of this man's mouth.

"Yes… that's my dog. His name is Titus," the man said, again in an aggressive tone.

"No. No, I think you're wrong, pal. You must have this dog mixed up with your dog," Tommy faced the man, his hands folded in front of him, and his shoulders squared.

"No way, man. That's my fucking dog!" The man raised his voice, "Someone stole him from outside a bar I was at about two weeks ago. That's definitely my dog. I paid thirty five hundred dollars for him, from a breeder in New Jersey, and he's got a chip in his neck that proves he's mine."

The man became more agitated. Tommy of course knew this was the dog's original owner, but repeated what he had just said.

"No, I don't think so, pal… You're making a mistake. This isn't your dog." He began to turn away from the man, and as he did, the man stepped forward, raising his voice even louder and reached out and grabbed Tommy's shoulder with his long arm.

"Hey! That's my fucking dog!" The man shouted at Tommy, now just two feet away.

Tommy quickly turned to face the man and threw a straight right hand, which landed right on the bridge of the man's nose, breaking it with an audible "Crack" and sending him straight to the concrete sidewalk on his back. Tommy, as quick as a cat, had his right knee on the sternum of the man's chest, and his left foot on the man's right arm, pinning him down to the sidewalk. Tommy's left hand still held onto little JoJo's leash and his right hand grabbed and tightened the Kufiya around the man's neck. The man covered his broken nose with his left hand as the blood ran into his well-kept beard. His eyes began to bug out of his head as the scarf tightened around his neck and Tommy began to speak in a low, but very forceful tone.

"Listen to me, you motherfucker. This is not your dog. Do you understand that? This is my fucking dog, and you know how I know this is my fucking dog? I can tell this is my dog because he's missing two of his fucking toes... Two fucking toes that were frozen off of the poor thing when some fucking cunt left him tied up to a fucking parking meter in five degree weather. So get this in your head, you fuck, this is not your fucking dog, and if you ever see this dog being walked by anyone in this neighborhood you better turn around, or cross to the other side of the street, you get that?" Tommy tightened the Kufiya even tighter, "Do you understand me?" he asked again, demanding an answer.

The man, obviously in quite a bit of pain and loaded with fear, nodded his head slightly and gurgled through the choking scarf and the blood that was filling his mouth.

"Yes."

Tommy stood up, removing his knee from the man's chest but still standing on the man's right arm. He lifted little JoJo from the sidewalk and tucked him under his right arm. Then, staring deeply into the tall man's eyes, he said, "I'm telling you... Stay away from me, and stay away from my dog."

Tommy then began to walk west again on 87th Street.

The man sat on the sidewalk, cupping the blood that was running from his badly bleeding broken nose with both hands. He mumbled something to the effect of "Fuck you."

Tommy, not quite sure what he heard, quickly turned around, again making eye contact with the man.

"I'm sorry, I'm sorry!" The man exclaimed, holding both blood covered hands up in the air, facing Tommy in the submissive "I don't want any trouble position," and shaking his head side to side.

Tommy again turned and began to walk back down 87th Street. As he approached the corner he said softly to himself, "No one's gonna fuck with my dog." Then, looking down at the little black and white dog tucked under his arm, he said to little JoJo, "That's right, you're my little dog, aren't you?" JoJo stuck his tongue out and caught Tommy on the lips with a dog kiss. "Okay, you're my dog, but no more of that, okay? I don't like the dog kisses, okay? Okay, you handsome little guy... my handsome little guy."

Epilogue

Herbert Abramson went to trial and was convicted on dozens of charges related to the kidnappings, and the death of Angela D'Amato. He was subsequently sentenced to 228 years and now sits in a cell in the Fishkill Correctional Facility in Beacon, NY.

Dalisay Beltran was also convicted on all charges, which also numbered in the dozens, and was subsequently sentenced to 174 years. She currently sits in a cell in the Bedford Hills Correctional Facility for Women, in Bedford Hills, New York.

Nineteen year-old Michael Booth, AKA Number One, was unable to be cared for by his mother, due to both his psychiatric state and his numerous physical needs. He currently resides at the Creedmoor Psychiatric Center in Queens Village, New York.

Seventeen year-old Samantha Moore, AKA Number Two, returned to live with her mother and grandmother on east 112th Street. She receives psychological and social work services from the city. Samantha still suffers with limited motor skills, as well as some organ issues, due to the effects of her malnutrition and it is believed she will never have an IQ of more than 40-50.

Fifteen year-old Jaime Aldeen, AKA Number Three, returned home to live with his mother, father, and older sister who now live in Wayne, New Jersey. He is enrolled in a private therapeutic day school for students with major emotional and psychiatric problems. As of yet, he is unable to recognize his family as his own.

The mummified body discovered in the trunk in the basement was positively identified through DNA testing to be that of Angela D'Amato, AKA the original Number Four. Her tiny body was laid to rest in Cavalry Cemetery in Queens, NY. She is survived by her mother, her father, and her two older sisters. Angela would have been thirteen years old. The Medical Examiner determined that she had died from a flu, and would have most certainly survived had she been taken to a hospital.

Eleven year-old Kieffer Blankenship, AKA Number Five, was identified and returned to the joint custody of his now divorced parents, who both reside on Manhattan's West Side. So far, he has not been enrolled in any sort of official school program, but does receive regular psychiatric counseling, as mandated by the courts and provided by the state.

Nine year-old Jennifer Bryan, AKA the second Number Four, lives with her father in Raleigh, North Carolina, with his new wife and their three dogs. She has gained enough weight to be considered normal-sized for a nine-year old. She still has some digestive and kidney problems due to her malnutrition, but her prognosis is considered to be good. Jennifer currently attends a day school for mentally deficient children, where she is excelling in all of her classes. Unfortunately, she will never know her mother, who was killed in a drunk driving accident on the Long Island Expressway, two years after Jennifer's abduction.

Seven year-old Tyler Winters, AKA Number Six, lives with his mother on East 54th Street. He has also not yet been enrolled into an official school program but has a good prognosis for both physical and mental recovery according to the doctors involved.

Five year-old Alexandria Monzos, AKA Number Seven, was returned to her family, who still lived in the same apartment on 99th Street and Third Avenue. She has been entered into a special program for underdeveloped preschoolers and has responded well to being back in her loving family's embrace, as well as to all physical and psychiatric testing that has been given to her.

Three year-old Hayden Jon Marshall, AKA Number Eight, was returned to his parents, and currently lives with his mother on East 79th Street. He suffered no visible psychological or physical harm during his abduction. His mother, Jessica, served his father, David, with divorce papers approximately four months after Hayden was rescued.

Derek Spree was convicted on hundreds of counts of child pornography, dozens of counts of trafficking, and three counts of rape in the first degree, under the New York State Penal Code. He was choked to death by a yet-unidentified inmate 92 days after his arrival at the Clinton Correctional facility in Dannemora, New York, and prior to any court appearances in the states of Virginia or Pennsylvania, where evidence had shown he had also raped children.

Charles Davenport was convicted on all charges in connection to his work with Derek Spree and the abduction and trafficking of at least six underage girls. He currently sits in a cell in USP (United States Penitentiary) in Allenwood, Pennsylvania, where he will spend the next 98 years, without possibility of parole.

The information uncovered and anonymously delivered to the NYPD by Roya Sarhadi, which led to the discovery of the A-P (All Pink) network, is still being unraveled and worked on by police departments across the country and in Canada. So far there have been over a dozen arrests of individuals involved in child pornography, kidnapping, and the rape of children, as young as four years of age in New York, Pennsylvania, Virginia, Washington DC, Toronto and Montreal.

***

All of this, however interesting, still awaits all participants in the future.

Currently, NYPD Detective Tommy Keane sleeps, awaiting his alarm to wake him to a new day, and for us to see whatever case The City of New York decides to hand him next.

Authors Note

In no way do the authors claim to be experts in computer hacking or in cybercrime.

And neither does Detective Tommy Keane, and that's why he has sought out the help of a professional.

Here is a little information to help you, the reader in the event that you, too, are clueless about the computer world. For those of you who are well informed on the subject, please forgive our ignorance.

Computer Hacking is an activity that looks to compromise digital devices such as computers, tablets, smart phones, as well as entire systems and networks.

Hackers typically use software and malware they refer to as tools, such as: Nmap, Metasploit, John The Ripper, and Wireshark just to name a few.

These and many other tools enable hackers to crack encrypted codes and enter into otherwise protected digital networks. People who write code tend to be very intelligent individuals, and therefore hackers who crack codes tend to also be exceptionally intelligent individuals.

Although the word hacker, to most, immediately sounds like a negative term, understand that is not the case. Hacking in and of itself is not an illegal act. What makes Hacking a crime is when one hacks into another system, network or device without permission.

Hackers are sometimes categorized as Black Hat, Grey Hat, and White Hat hackers.

Black Hat Hackers: As you would expect the Black Hat hacker, as in an old west film, is the bad guy. These individuals or groups tend to seek criminal financial gain from their hacks or commit some sort of corporate or governmental espionage.

White Hat Hackers: Also called Ethical Hackers, attempt to improve the security of an organization's digital network by finding vulnerabilities in systems in an attempt to stop cybercrimes, such as identity theft, by finding and securing flaws in the systems they themselves are hacking. Most all large corporations and governments employ White Hat Hackers to protect their networks.

Grey Hat Hackers: These hackers walk the line between the two. They may hack a system and then point out its flaws to the owner in hopes of a reward, or to repair it for a fee. Many may also see themselves as Hacktavists, who, although illegally hack without permission, justify it as hacking for a cause.

The Dark Web: This is part of the internet that isn't indexed by search engines, and it is a virtual hotbed of criminal activity, where up to 60% of its sites host illicit material. It is a haven for smugglers of drugs and weapons, child pornographers, and human traffickers, who use TOR (The Onion Router) browsers to anonymize their web traffic, thereby protecting their illegal activities online.

Travis Myers & Natasha Myers Marsiguerra

Hayden Jon Marshall

Read on for a sneak peek at the next book in the Tommy Keane series:

JENNY BLACK

4:12 pm John Finley Walk, Carl Schurz Park

Detectives Keane and Colletti arrived at Carl Schurz Park and found two patrol cars parked on John Finley Walk, the promenade that bordered and looked out over the East River.

Tommy and Jimmy exited their vehicle and as they did Sergeant Diaz, a tall, slim, dark skinned man with his hair slicked straight back exited his. He placed his hat on his head, straightening it just so before he approached the detectives.

"Afternoon, Sergeant, what you guys got for us?" Tommy asked.

"Afternoon guys…Cold enough for yous?" The Sergeant replied, "There's a body of what looks like a young woman just over the rail here…here, come take a look." Sergeant Diaz motioned with his head toward the direction of the river and the iron railing that ran along it. He walked the detectives around his patrol car and pointed over the edge, "You'll have to step up on the railing and look down."

Both Tommy and Jimmy stepped up onto the crunchy ice covered snow that the plow had left and then put a foot onto the rails cross bracing and lifted themselves up and onto the rail. They both looked down and saw a young woman partially covered in snow. Half of her face and black hair was exposed, her left arm and gloved hand, as well as part of her left leg and boot were visible, the rest of her was shrouded in snow.

"Jesus!" Jimmy exclaimed, "How are we supposed to examine the body?" he asked.

The woman's body lay on a concrete and stone abutment that stuck out about 5-6 feet from the continuous wall that came up from the East River to the promenade. Looking over the rail, one could see there were a handful of these abutments that protruded somewhat randomly along the stone wall and would only be visible if one were to lean over the railing to see them, or from a boat out on the river.

"Well, it's not that far, Jimmy, we can climb down and take a look, fuck I wish everything wasn't covered in snow and ice." Tommy replied to Jimmy's question and he threw one leg over the rail and then the other.

"Tommy…what are you crazy, if you fall into the water you'll be dead before we can pull you out from hypothermia!" Jimmy protested.

"Relax, I'll be fine. There's plenty of room here." He dropped himself down the six or so feet onto the abutment the center of which seemed to be about six or seven feet wide and then triangled itself back to the walls at either end over a span of maybe 20 feet.

Tommy landed soundly in the twelve inch snow drift that had piled up against the stone wall, shouted up to Jimmy and Sergeant Diaz.

"Has the Medical Examiner been notified? … also give ESU a call. Let's see if they have some equipment that can help us retrieve this young lady…Fuck, I wish I wore some proper boots today…Put a call into crime scene as well please, I don't want to get to close or disturb her body until we have the okay from everyone."

"You think she's a homicide, Tom?" Jimmy shouted down to Tommy.

"No way to tell," Tommy replied, squatting next to the body, he poked it gently. "She's frozen solid though, completely solid…no way to know right now until after crime scene and the medical examiner show, could be a homicide, possibly she tried to jump into the river and landed here instead then froze, maybe a drug or alcohol fueled accident? … no way to tell or even make a guess right now."

Tommy stared at what was visible of the body, and the scene that surrounded it.

Young female 20-25 years of age. Nice looking face, the one eye that was not covered by the snow and was visible was wide open and brown. She wore makeup; her eyebrows were manicured, dark red almost maroon lipstick, jet black hair with one blue highlight that was noticeable. On her body was a black Alpha brand nylon MA-1 flight jacket zipped up to the top over what appeared to be a black hooded sweatshirt, black skintight denim jeans cuffed up to show off her black Dr. Martens 1490 boots.

After about six minutes Tommy shouted up, "Okay, I'm coming back up." He jumped up to grab the edge of the stone wall but slipped off, then tried a second time and was able to hang on long enough to pull himself high enough to reach the iron railing and then pull himself all the way up and climb over the top of the railing back onto the promenade.

"You're a fuckin' nut." Jimmy stated flatly.

"Hey, we gotta see what's going on here, Jimmy, how else was I supposed to take a look." Tommy replied, as his body shuddered from the cold, "Let's get back in the car and wait for the others to arrive."

Sergeant Diaz was already tucked back into his patrol car and Tommy and Jimmy climbed into their vehicle as well to ward off the cold. Tommy sat silently and made some notes in his notebook and then took the notes Jimmy had made.

"Did Sergeant Diaz say who discovered the body?" Tommy asked

"Yeah, it was a 911 call from a passing boat that said they saw what looked like a body lying there in the snow, and that was earlier in the day, I guess it took the patrol guys a couple looks to find it, I can see why, who would think to ever look there, especially on a day like today." Jimmy replied.

***

First to show was a truck from the NYPD Emergency Services Truck 2, but they couldn't do anything until crime scene and the medical examiner's office were finished with the body.

Second, about 30-40 minutes later, crime scene arrived to the park. They set up their equipment and started to take photographs and measurements. Emergency Service helped out by supplying a couple of ladders, some rigging and two large spotlights that lit up the abutment brighter than daylight, as it was now dark out. They used the rigging to tie everything together and make everyone's work a little safer than attempting the climb Tommy had made earlier.

Finally the medical examiner's office made its appearance, Jimmy immediately making note of it for the unusual report.

"Oh, look who's here; do you know what we call her?" Jimmy asked.

A tall attractive woman, with slicked back blond hair and a very long black wool coat, high heeled boots, and a stainless steel document case exited her vehicle and looked toward the detectives.

"The Vampire." Tommy answered.

"Oh…so you know her?" Jimmy replied, slightly disappointed he didn't get to share that bit of information.

Tommy and Jimmy exited their vehicle and walked toward the woman, meeting her half way.

"Evening, M.E. Marcus, how you doing today?" Tommy asked.

"Not bad, a bit cold, Detective…Keane, correct?" She most certainly knew exactly who Tommy was from past cases.

"Yes, you are correct."

Both had worked on numerous homicides together in the past, but Ms. Marcus had a stone cold, matter of fact, way of speaking , that she always seemed dismissive and borderline rude, however she was without a doubt one of the premiere examiners at the ME's office.

She walked ahead of the detectives over to where the rail was and the ladders that went up and over it.

"So what do we have? A jumper?" She asked.

"We have no idea," Tommy replied, "Young woman, I'd say early twenties, mostly covered in snow and she's frozen solid."

Angela Marcus attempted to look over the rail, and then realized she couldn't see from that vantage point so she did as Tommy and Jimmy did and stepped up on the rail and peered over. In her matter of fact monotone voice she stated, "She's dead," Then stepped down and made her way over to the ladders.

"Are you ok? Will you need a hand?" Officer Dowd from Emergency Services asked.

"No thank you, Officer, I'll be fine."

She unbuttoned her long wool coat, then climbed the 3-4 rungs of the first ladder and swung her right leg over to the second. She looked like a swashbuckling pirate climbing a tall ships rigging from some old Hollywood film as her long coat blew in the wind. Once she was down, Tommy followed her and the remaining crime scene officer removed himself from the scene saying, "We're pretty much done here, let me get out of your way and give you some more room so none of us fall into the drink." Then he climbed back up the ladder.

Marcus surveyed the area and then the body while Tommy surveyed both the body and Marcus as she made her initial exam. He watched Marcus to see if he could see what was going on in her mind through her facial expressions and eye movements. Tommy got nothing from Marcus though, she was like a poker champion and there was nothing to read on her face. She wasn't trying to keep anything from Tommy, it was just her way.

She scrapped the snow and ice off the body as best she could, and attempted to feel through the young woman's jacket and pants.

"She seems to be frozen solid, which unfortunately means we won't be able to do an autopsy for at least a week until she thaws out completely...I'm sure you understand or realize there's nothing we can do about that, to properly thaw a body, frozen like this will, most certainly take about seven days...from what I can see here I can't tell you much, Detective...let's take her up top to the pavement where we can flip her and I can give a more thorough examination of her clothing, and maybe a better look at her body."

They left the girl's body and made their way back up to the pavement. The Emergency Service officers took over and dropped a basket down to pull the body up, and then along with a couple of guys from patrol, pulled the young woman's body up and over the rail.

Angela Marcus took another look at the body, slowly and deliberately brushing off all the snow. She searched the body, along with Tommy, for any bullet or knife holes in her clothing; they then flipped the stiff body over and did the same along her back, carefully looking for any holes or clues. Once they were satisfied there were none, they again flipped the body back onto its back.

Angela Marcus unzipped the young woman's outer jacket and looked it over for any signs of damage; she then unbuttoned the black denim vest that was under it, and finally the zippered hooded sweatshirt that the girl had worn over a t-shirt. M.E. Marcus then stood from her squat and looked directly at Tommy.

"I'm sorry, Detective, I really won't be able to tell you anything today, I, as you, see no visible wounds, no visible broken bones, this here in the eye appears to be a slight Petechiae which could be from any number of reasons, but in this frozen state it will take a full autopsy to tell you more about her cause of death…here is my card, may I have yours please, I will call you before the autopsy so you can come witness it."

About the Authors

Travis Myers and Natasha Myers Marsiguerra are a brother and sister team who both grew up in New York City.

Travis is a retired New York City Police Detective, and Natasha works for the IBEW (International Brotherhood of Electrical Workers) Local 234 in California.

Together they form a perfect team in that Travis, who has more stories to tell than a pub full of Irishmen, suffers from dyslexia and abhors anything to do with reading or writing. Natasha, his beloved little sister, is an avid reader of absolutely anything that is put in front of her and has been blessed with the gift of gab. She can out-story just about anyone, in any room, at any given time, and she can also type 60 words per minute. More importantly, Natasha is able to understand where her older brother is coming from, and craft his stories into a readable format.

Together, they weave the Tommy Keane Detective series into well-braided fictional tales that are nearly all based in actual events that they, and their friends and relatives, have lived. Travis and Natasha deliver on their promise to tell gritty, honest stories that are rooted in the everyday lives of everyday people.

Hayden Jon Marshall

CPSIA information can be obtained
at www.ICGtesting.com
Printed in the USA
FSHW010631041120
75428FS

9 781734 337037